The Bexford North/Annie Watson Mystery series
comprise six books, each complete in itself:

1. *And The Dance Goes On*

2. *The Black Lamb*

3. *The Blight of Lady Emily*

4. *The Bell Tolled Twice*

5. *Death and the Lazy Milkmaid*

6. *Death and the Dowagers*

DEATH AND THE LAZY MILKMAID

BEXFORD NORTH, SYDNEY – WINTER 1944

TONY BRENNAN

ISBN: 978-1-925681-34-5

Published by Vivid Publishing
P.O. Box 948, Fremantle
Western Australia 6959
www.vividpublishing.com.au

Cataloguing-in-Publication data is available from the National Library of Australia

ACKNOWLEDGEMENTS

To Doctor PSB for long hours spent in boring revision and proof-reading of my work, my sincere and genuine gratitude.

To those grand people of the war years who shared their memories of the period with me: the dignity, compassion; their care for each other, amid personal and national disasters, remains a treasured source of admiration.

I wish to honour, especially, those glorious, heroic farmers who kept the essential food supply going – with most of their workers away at war.

***

I wish to acknowledge Mark Felton's great book: '*Japan's Gestapo*', 2009. This writer gave me a splendid insight into the mind-set of the Japanese soldiers which became apparent in the Pacific Campaign in which Australian forces were heavily engaged, resulting in horrific casualties.

DEDICATION

This one is for Michael K.

FOREWORD

In this 21st century where food is available in every supermarket in every town – no matter how small; where meat is plentiful, often hygienically-wrapped in certified amounts; where milk is available in multiple plastic bottles on shelves; where fruit is piled high on counters, washed, waxed and shiny – where everything is shiningly clean, hygienic and in great abundance, it is difficult to understand that there could ever be a time – such a relatively, short time ago – when not only to procure the above items, but to actually *produce* them, involved great hardship: much sweat, intense hard work, long days working under a relentless sun, or enduring soaking rain, as a normal working event; where, in fact, life working on a farm, with no sophisticated, computerized equipment, was an activity which required heroic mental endurance, immense physical strength and the ability to endure every calamity known to man – especially the two perpetual threats to Australian farmers: Droughts and Floods.

Farming has never been easy. Farmers are the salt of the earth; they need to be both strong physically and mentally. In Australia, farmers have always had to work very hard; our very geography, our great distances, our harsh climate all make for a difficult and demanding life.

With WW2, farmers were, on the whole, an 'exempt occupation' – after all, people don't stop eating just because there is a war; the food has to keep coming. As Australia was so richly blessed with productive soil – around its Eastern borders, at least – it very soon was required not only to feed its own people and its army, but also to save England from starving to death.

This meant that farmers had to work twice as long, and as hard, as they had previously done. To add to their problems was the number of their employees who ran off to 'join up'; to volunteer for the Army, as did many of their sons and daughters as well. This left the farmers in a terrible situation: they had the gigantic task of feeding the multitudes with a fraction of the workforce they'd employed before the war and then, at that time, they had only half as many for whom they had to provide.

Dairy Farming is, as most people know, the most demanding – in terms of non-stop work – of all farming. It is a 24/7 programme. To assist with the fearsome situation when dairy farmers and their wives were reaching near-total exhaustion, the Government introduced the Land Army Girls, as a special force, under the control of the Department of Defence. They were sent to the farmers who requested them. Many of these young women, however, had never before worked on a farm; they had no idea of the intense labour involved. These Land Army Girls were not introduced until late in the war, and regardless of experience, or lack thereof, they were a tremendous help to the men and women trying to hold a farm together.

The situation I have created with Hannah Kelly and her son, Dan, was a typical situation that you would have found all around this country. Hannah with her steel corsets was typical of those valiant women who, no matter how they personally suffered, joined their husbands, or sons, in order to try desperately to have something to hand on to their children when they came back – *if* they came back – when the war eventually ended.

The farmers of Australia were heroic; they deserve our admiration and our respect. The Land Army Girls also were a glorious and, largely neglected and forgotten, part of the Australian Army history. In WW2 they forged a proud tradition of service.

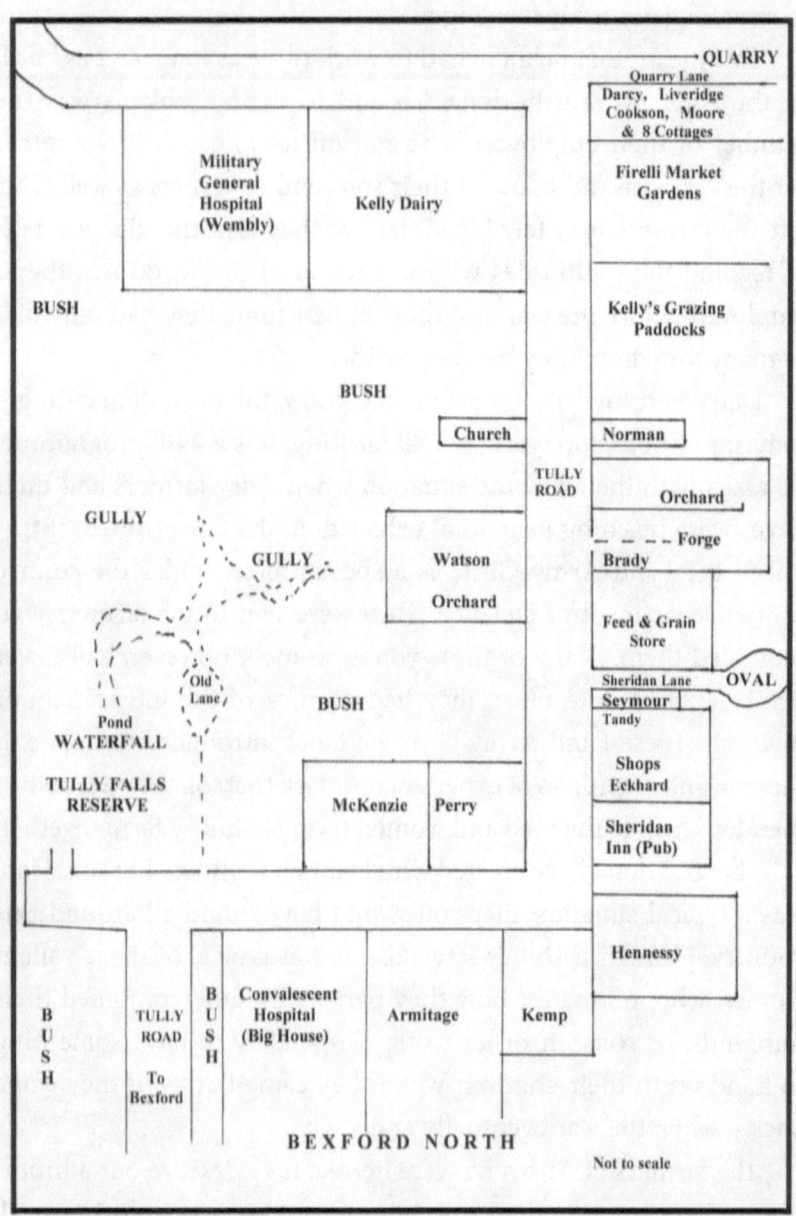

ONE

The freezing winter wind found its way through the wooden slats of the milking shed, causing the kerosene lanterns to sway precariously, their glass chimneys rattling ominously.

Dan Kelly shivered, pulling his thick knitted beanie down even lower, almost covering his eyebrows; he was grateful for the two sweaters under his overalls and the thick woolly socks in his old Wellington boots. His thick muscular arms were shovelling the mixture of fodder; it would go into the tin troughs in front of each stall, so the cows could feed as they were milked.

Dan worked quickly and as he had been doing this, for as long as he could remember, it was now almost automatic.

He was vaguely aware that his mother was late – she was usually down by now. As he went to the paddock gate to call the cows, he found most of them waiting, their breaths steaming in the cold air.

A blast of wind hit him, so he hurried to get the milking started; the cows would then shield him from the wind.

Back at the farm house, Hannah Kelly, a big, raw-boned, Irish woman, was muttering to herself as she struggled to finish dressing. "Wretched steel corsets; they're the absolute limit, but needs must!" Dr Kemp had ordered her to wear them; that was the end of the matter.

Corsets finally in place, the winter cold hurried her into piling on warm clothing.

From the moaning sound rattling the old house, the wind was obviously severe, so Hannah pulled on a beanie – it would be bitterly cold down in the sheds. As she dressed, her ears were alert for any other sounds of movement in the house.

She was suddenly, acutely aware, of the silence in the house. She frowned. Where the hell were those two wretched girls? They should be down there helping Dan before they started milking.

Hannah thought with gratitude of Annie Watson's suggestion.

It was Annie who had suggested the Land Army Girls as a way to help the frightful situation Hannah and Dan were in, with the twins, Sean and Patrick, sent away to war.

It had certainly saved the situation at the farm. Hannah thought, wryly, it probably saved my sanity as well.

Her thoughts were interrupted by a crashing bang as Sally, the fat girl, banged out of her room, followed by the sound of running feet. Well, that's one of them out of the bed-clothes, anyhow. She'll get the edge of Dan's tongue for being late, but where's the other one?

If she's slept in again, I'll deal with her – the useless, posturing, lazy, miserable wretch! Why ever *she* volunteered for farm work is beyond belief; her rightful place is in a beauty parlour buffeting idle, rich people's nails. That's all she's good for, the useless creature.

Hannah hurried even more now, as she realised that Jean, the second girl, had obviously slept in, so she, herself, would be needed urgently by Dan; he'll be at his wit's end by this time.

Her eyes slid to the clock. It was already past four o'clock. They'd never get the lot milked in time if she didn't hurry. I'll just dash into that tart's room, drag the bed clothes from her, threaten her with dismissal, then run down to the milking shed.

As Hannah left the room she noticed that the blackout blind had been slightly crooked; it would have shown a light when she first got out of bed as the alarm clock went off.

Normally that would have worried her – everyone was now absolutely scrupulous about the blackout, but today, Hannah felt rebellious. Let the bloody Japs bomb us and get it over with! How many more years are we to cope with this?

Running stiffly to Jean's room, Hannah, throwing the door wide, with her mouth open to start a harangue which would have blistered the paint from the walls, was left staring at the empty room – the bed hadn't been slept in.

Hannah quickly looked in the wardrobe, thinking the wretched girl had done a secret flit in the night, but again paused, bewildered. The closet was full of clothes, the girl's suitcases were still in their usual place; her jewellery was in the little crystal dish on the dressing table.

She really isn't here, Hannah realised; she hasn't been here all night. Well, that finishes it, she decided. I'm sending her away the moment she comes back – I won't put up with her for another minute and I'll demand the Army send me another girl to replace her.

Otherwise the bloody, demanding Army can whistle for their damn milk! Dan and I can't perform miracles.

With her lips tightly pressed together Hannah made her way down the yard to the milking shed, aware now she was outside the house, of the intensity of the cold wind; she heard the cows' lowing, while they waited for relief from the pressure of their milk.

But first, she'd have to tell Dan. He'll swear and carry on, but perhaps that'll be a good thing, better than just bottling it up inside. What a mess! However, young fatty will just have to take her share of the extra cows to milk.

She'd signed on for this job, so there's no special favours going here: the Army demands the milk; they've taken two of my boys away, yet they expect one young man and an old woman like me, to carry on as if nothing has happened! Bloody idiots!

Hannah found young Dan looking furious as he milked and swearing at a recalcitrant cow. He admitted, sourly, that he had already heard of Jean's absence – the other one had told him.

Hannah was relieved as she noticed Sally keeping quiet, with her head down and milking more energetically than usual; it was clear she expected fireworks to come when the milking was over. Hannah went to the dairy room; collected the buckets she needed: the milk bucket and a water bucket and cloth to wash the udders.

She opened the turnstile to let in another batch of cows; only then could she go to her usual position and found, as she expected, the leading cow already in position and waiting for her.

Without even being consciously aware of doing so, Hannah tied the leg rope, slipped the bail closed, pulled the stool over, buried her head in the side of the cow, and began milking – even faster than usual – aware of the lateness of the hour.

It was now half past four o'clock on a mercilessly cold, frosty winter's morning.

TWO

Standing at the window of his bedroom, the murderer watched the dawn break. He had been unable to sleep, his mind skittering back and forth, as he saw her face, again and again; gasping, trying desperately to breathe.

It had taken him longer than he had realised to kill her; he thought it would have been over much quicker. He heard himself muttering again: "Die, why *won't* you die?"

He saw again the last look she had given him; he stepped back quickly from the window, his heart thudding painfully in his chest. Even with her last ounce of strength, she had looked at him with hatred – her eyes locked on his.

After it was finally over, he had stared with loathing at the face of the dead girl, speaking aloud: "You stupid bitch; we could've had a life together."

He found his hands were shaking. Stop it, his mind screamed; it's over! He'd kept his nerve; he'd actually done it! Done it, as he'd been ordered and done it *happily* – she'd deserved every moment of it!

She'd been rotten – rotten to the core. She's gone forever now; she'd never do that to him again – or to any other man.

He was suddenly aware of the cold morning wind and shivered. He was also shockingly aware he had to face the coming day with whatever it brought. He'd better have another shower and put on clean clothes – he might feel better. He had to face people, as if it were just another day.

It would never be just like another day for him, for the rest of his life.

THREE

"Stand still, you stupid beast," Hannah Kelly ordered in her loud voice, as she bent to tie the leg-rope on yet another cow. "Any more nonsense from you and you'll find yourself going for a ride in Fred Tanby's lorry; you won't be coming back either."

The cow, suitably admonished and ready to eat the oats in front of her, relaxed her udder and let Hannah's old fingers automatically strip the milk into the frothing bucket, which she held firmly between her legs as she sat on the milking stool.

Hannah winced as the sharp pain pierced through her back again. Getting old, she muttered; how much longer is it possible to keep going, I wonder? The corsets will help; hope so anyway.

However, it doesn't matter; we *must* keep going – no alternative. There must be *something* left for Sean, when he comes home – *if* he comes home – please, please, God have mercy.

And, for Patrick, too; wherever he is and wherever those little yellow people have got him in their filthy camp. *Japanese*! I've never ever even met a Japanese! Now my baby is in their clutches. And the papers say they are monsters! The things they say they do, to their prisoners!

They surely don't, do they? They wouldn't, would they? Oh God, God, God, bring him home alive, *please, please, please* – he's just a boy. Holy Mother, don't let them kill him.

Hannah suddenly remembered what they did to that poor black

American boy, Louis, who had been at the Convalescent Hospital! God in Heaven, don't let them do that to Patrick! And, where is that poor black boy now? He'd be fighting again somewhere in the Pacific, as well – the unfeeling, merciless Army would have sent him back to the Japanese hell that had nearly sent him insane in the first place!

Haven't they any pity? ... Yes, the Pacific – that's where the Americans are fighting. The papers say the Japs are massing in Rabaul – I wonder where that is? Somewhere near New Guinea, she thought vaguely.

They say the whole area is swarming with those little people now: people who are so cruel, so fiendishly cruel – inhuman! Inhuman, yes that's what they are! ... Bloody pagans, as well!

The cow gave a soft, protesting sound. "And what's wrong with you now, you silly old woman?" Hannah demanded, then realised that the cow had given all the milk she had and was letting her know she was finished. Hannah's sense of fairness returned, and she stopped milking, washed the udder with the wet cloth and stood up, holding one hand to her back.

"Sorry, old girl. Not your fault, mine. You're a good old faithful one; shouldn't have blasted you," She patted the side of the cow as she released the leg-rope, undid the bail, and let the old cow find its own way back to the outside paddock.

Meanwhile Dan had kept the feed coming, as well as doing his own share of milking and Hannah saw that there was a new bucket of oats and hay in the trough, as the next cow walked into the stall. How many is that? Hannah wondered. We must be nearly done, surely, even without the help of that blasted lazy trollop.

A trollop! Yes, that's what she is. She's been out all night and could be anywhere now with some bloke or other, you can be sure of that. Perhaps the Land Army girls was not such a good idea, after all.

Sighing wearily, Hannah picked up another full bucket of milk and trudged to the dairy room where she poured it into one of the large cans, ready on the trolley, for collection by the Army milk requisition truck.

It made its appearance, every morning and evening, with the inevitability of night following day. Dan and Hannah called it, with grim humour, their daily reminder of human mortality!

FOUR

Mrs Elise Seymour, a tall thin woman with a pinched look, tightly permed black hair and small, round metal-framed spectacles, had risen early and was happily wandering through her new home, hardly believing her good fortune.

She was now living in the beautiful village of Bexford North – the village she had coveted since she had first heard that it was exclusive, refined with only the socially 'acceptable' living there – which, of course, was only half true.

In her daily tour of the house, Elise lingered in her front parlour – she loved this room: its richness and obvious affluence, pleased her immensely; it would be a clear sign to her new neighbours of just how wealthy, they really were.

Elise heard sounds of the family waking and went, happily, to her spotless kitchen. Before starting on the breakfast, Elise looked with satisfaction at the gleaming tiles, the brand new electric stove and the hot water tank over the sink.

She had never dreamed she would have hot water on tap, whenever she wanted it – this was luxury! No more lugging hot water from the temperamental geyser in the bathroom! Oh, everything now modern, brand new and shiningly beautiful!

Well, of course, she would still have to pretend – to others – that the war was a terrible, terrible thing but, as far as she was concerned, with the wonderful job her husband had – the war had been a godsend! Nothing was going to spoil their new life she resolved firmly – absolutely nothing!

FIVE

Breakfast at the Kellys became a silent affair, after Hannah had spoken her piece to Sally Flinders, the plump Land Army Girl. Sally ate her breakfast hungrily, but was sulkily aware that her colleague, that idiot girl, Jean, had placed her in a frightful situation.

Sally knew that Jean was meeting someone last night and had promised not to tell, but under the wrath of Hannah's tongue, had finally admitted she did know that Jean was meeting a man and, yes, it was possible that she had spent the night with him.

After that admission, Sally refused utterly to say another word. The meal progressed as usual. It was a big meal, well deserved after hours of work.

Hannah usually left the milking fifteen minutes, or so, earlier than the others and by the time they had cleaned the shed and then themselves, they were ready for the hot meal she had waiting for them – having prepared everything the night before.

In such demanding work as a dairy farm, there was no time to waste sitting about, or not planning each, and every activity. It all had to work like clockwork. The cows were demanding taskmasters.

Hannah and Dan discussed the work of the day ahead of them and the vexed problem of whether or not to inoculate those two cows, which were under the weather.

The threat of mastitis was always present; Dan had become an experienced amateur vet in the years he had worked with the cows.

That topic finished, Hannah reverted to the missing girl at the end of the meal.

Her anger had dissipated and she was starting to worry. After all, the stupid girl was only a youngster and it could be said, she was under, in some way, Hannah's protection.

"Is it possible, Dan, that some harm has come to that dratted girl? Should we give Inspector Peters a ring, do you think?"

"Surely not after only one night, Mum," Dan replied, "but if she doesn't turn up today, I suppose we'll have to notify someone," He turned to face Sally; they did not like each other, but were polite, as people have to be, who have no alternative when working together. "Sally, what do you think? You've said you knew Jean was meeting someone. Is she safe do you think? Should we contact the police?"

"For the love of Mike! No!" Sally almost shouted. "Surely to God a girl who's over twenty-one can go missing for one night, without the bloody cavalry being called in."

"Well, she's not getting another chance, and that's final," Hannah declared loudly. "I'm ringing the Milk Inspector this morning; I'll be demanding he arrange for another girl. I'll not put up with immorality in this house."

Sally rose from the table, her face furious. "While you're about it, Mrs Kelly, ask him for *two* girls, not one. I want out of this place. I don't mind the work but with all the praying and pious bullshit going on here, I don't want another minute of it,"

Sally took a deep breath. "And another thing: I don't like you, Mrs Kelly with your loud, boisterous voice and your pious humbug; as for your son, the precious Daniel, I wouldn't be Bianca for a million quid. She might just as well be marrying a toad; a man with no sex appeal at all, a two-faced, hypocritical Mummy's boy, who has no mind of his own to speak of at all."

Hannah listened, her face turning scarlet. Dan had risen in his chair and was staring at the girl, his eyes growing large with anger. He raised his hand, only to be quickly grabbed by his mother.

"No, Dan, that's what she's trying to make you do," Hannah shook her son roughly. "Dan, listen to me! Go and attend to the cows – they need to go out to the lucerne pasture that's just been baled. They'll get a good feed from the stubble that's left but only keep them there for an hour at the most, so there'll be no danger of them getting bloat."

Dan hesitated, then, with his face black with suppressed rage, left the table without a word, slamming the door on his way out.

Hannah turned to the girl. "Now you, girl, go to your room. Pack your things and get out. I'll give you exactly one hour to get everything ready; if you're not out of my house by then, I'll personally throw you out."

Hannah's spoke quietly this time, but the tone was of such suppressed violence, that Sally realised she had gone too far. She risked one look at the face of the older woman, which made her realise there was no turning back now. She scrambled from her chair and ran to her room.

Right! That's relieved my feelings, Hannah commented dryly to herself as she sat down, her hands shaking, but now it's a bloody catastrophe!

There's no one now, except Dan and me to do everything. Oh, I could kill that blasted Jean – she's caused all this; we've managed to get on – even if we didn't like each other – up to this time, but now! Jean, Jean, bloody, bloody useless Jean! And, *WHERE* the hell *is* the young, troublesome woman who caused this problem, anyhow?

SIX

In fact, Jean was not far away at all.

Sheridan Lane was a short road leading to the village oval. There was only one building in the lane – the Feed and Grain store: a large, old, rambling structure, with a disused annexe to one side.

The store sold just about everything the farmers needed. It also had a comprehensive, if haphazardly arranged, supply of hardware merchandise as well. On the outside wall was an old fashioned loading device – as it was called – which resembled a portcullis. It was a section of the old timber wall that could be let down on chains to form a solid platform three feet from the ground. There were two large and powerful pointed hooks attached to chains, inside the structure, which, through the use of ratchets, could be lowered and raised to lift heavy bales of hay and bags of feed to the waiting vehicles outside the store.

It was an odd arrangement, but it worked. It enabled the two men, no longer young, who owned the store, to manage the heavy tasks they faced every day. Each evening, the platform was pulled up, to become once more, a part of the outside wall.

Just to one side of the loading device was another relic of the past: a long, deep, stone water-trough built originally for the convenience of horses to slake their thirst.

When the owners of the store, the two Munroe brothers, both elderly, terribly correct but dithery, remembered the trough, they cleaned it out and filled it with clean water.

However, it had not been cleaned throughout the whole of the past summer, and was now coated with thick green slime. Being close to Tully Road, on the way from the pub, the water level had risen from time to time as drunken soldiers used it, on their way back to the Military Hospital at Wembley Park.

It smelt to high heaven and customers had complained frequently to the owners of the store, always to be assured, courteously, that it would be attended to as soon as time permitted.

The Munroe bachelor brothers, Charlie and Eric, sincerely meant to clean the old trough and were, in fact, very proud of it; it had stood on the same spot since 1862 when the firm was founded by their grandfather.

The problem was that they only remembered it whenever they happened to come out the front door of the store, but as they were usually so very busy in the big structure, they forgot the trough as soon as they re-entered the building.

Living in the back section of the store, the smell never reached them, when they turned in, after a hard day's work.

The body of a young woman was submerged in the green slime, but it had displaced a lot of water which was now lying on the concrete beneath.

The trough was not in an exposed position, but with the day's cold wind blowing strongly, it disturbed the water which, in turn, caused the body to roll from side to side, except for one arm which had been caught in cadaveric spasm and remained stiff as a board. From time to time, the hand was held up in the air above the water.

With the movement of the water, it seemed to be beckoning the onlooker to come closer and closer.

It was an eleven year old boy, named Alexander Seymour who, on his way to school, was sufficiently intrigued to see a hand apparently waving to him, from the filthy trough, to investigate this curious phenomenon.

SEVEN

Alexander Montague Seymour was an unpleasant child. He sported, proudly, a very large boil on the back of his neck, which made him feel a real man, as so many men – through poor wartime diet – had boils now where their collars rubbed their necks.

Alexander's eyes were small and close together; his face narrow, while the mouth was small with his upper teeth protruding over his lower lip.

In character, he answered Shakespeare's query as to whether a person's character could be discerned in the face – in a resounding affirmative.

Alexander was unpleasant without and within. He told lies without the slightest compunction, listened sneakily to private conversations and was the first to tell tales on others. He appeared to care for no one but himself.

He had a vivid imagination, fed from the forbidden, questionable books and magazines he read secretly, also from the 'movies' – he, now, used the American word for the Pictures and despised anybody who referred to them otherwise.

Alexander preferred the Chicago, gangster-type movies; he copied the characters' manner of speaking as well as their vocabulary. His dubious reading was shared within a wild group of older boys with money that mysteriously appeared when needed. As Alexander could always be depended on to have money on him, he was permitted to join the older gang – even though he was only eleven.

Elise Seymour, Alexander's mother, was blind to any fault in her best loved child. She believed, implicitly, that with names such as Alexander and Montague it simply was impossible to conceive how her boy could ever go wrong, or not have a great destiny.

Her youngest son, Jason, was still too young to be of much interest, being only four, while twelve-year-old Diana was a sore disappointment. She was quiet, introverted, decidedly plain, who found it impossible to make friends and had developed acne.

To her mother's despair, Diana, so inappropriately named, hung her head when addressed by neighbours; mumbling when questioned.

Elise, to her husband Gerald's amusement, was determined, now that they had settled in the decidedly 'posh' Bexford North, to be one with the 'gentry'.

However, apart from Alexander, she did not see her children as helping in the process.

Elise wanted to see herself as one with the ladies of the village; involved in all their affairs, listened to, invited to everything and in great demand. Her greatest dread was to be thought 'common' – she had worked hard on her speech and cringed when either she, or one of her family, forgot and spoke 'uncouthly' – as poor Elise called it.

Elise had realised that just being wealthy was not enough; she had to become 'genteel' as well. To this end she warned Gerald that they were never to mention the fact that they had previously lived in the inner city, in a rough area.

In all, Elise had found her husband of little help; he had no interest in her social ambitions, so she had set her hopes on Alexander; he would be the one who would fulfil all her ambitions. He would do splendidly at school; he could, perhaps, even become a lawyer or a doctor. Poor Elise imagined herself, in the future, introducing her son, 'My son, Dr Seymour'. She dreamed of the day she would hold an enviable position in village society – be seen as someone like that Annie Watson woman. When that happened, every door would open before her.

Jerry – as he preferred to be called – thought his wife was laughable, but it behoved him to comply, at least outwardly, with her pretensions, for he was engaged in a number of activities that were most definitely *not* social desirable!

He had settled in well in Bexford North and set out to make himself agreeable. He was very shrewd with finance and quick to seize a bargain. He had been delighted to buy their new home – a beautiful stone cottage, as soon as it came on the market, paying cash for the property – which imbued the Estate Agent with deep suspicions.

However, Jerry had seen, at a glance, the future value of the property, which was a gem. He was popular with the men at the pub, where he was seen most nights of the week – being generous to a fault in buying drinks.

He was good looking, dressed well and was polite and courteous to the women of the village, who responded with customary caution – as they did to all newcomers.

He even went so far as to accompany his wife, the squirming Alexander – with the other two children – to Mr Norman's Church each Sunday. Elise had made it quite clear that this was essential, in her quest for respectability.

Poor Elise wanted to dress as she imagined was expected of her in her new social position, so wore her dresses longer than usual – mid-calf – but, for some reason, made of the smallest quantity of material possible. As Elise was painfully thin, she often looked – as Sam Watson had once confided, uncharitably, to Annie his wife – the poor woman reminded him of a tightly wrapped oyster bottle.

Such was the family that now lived in the house of the dearly loved previous owner, Amelia Tatley. The family had created a little buzz of excitement when they had moved in, but it was mainly because of the history of the house.

Since then, however, apart from the friendliness of Annie Watson – their neighbour opposite – they had been largely ignored.

But, now they were to be in the limelight in a way that neither husband nor wife desired in the slightest – but for entirely different reasons.

EIGHT

When Alexander went across to the water-trough he saw that it *was* a human hand sticking out of the slimy water. He noted that the water had dripped from the hand and the nails were a bright red, where they had been painted, so the body had to be a woman.

The boy realised that he was looking at a dead body; it appeared so similar to the movies he had seen, it didn't seem real.

The fact that the woman was dead he didn't find frightening, but on the contrary, rather exciting. Wait till I tell the others at school about this, raced through his head! He could hardly wait until he got there to tell them, but, perhaps, he had better find out more about the body first.

He hesitated a moment, then putting on his 'Chicago gangster's face' from the movies, he realised that he didn't have much time on his own with the body – some busybody 'grown-up' could come along any minute. When they did, they'd spoil all the fun and send him, as a kid, flying, so Alex decided to act while he had the chance.

Taking hold of the hand, the boy pulled it toward him. This caused the body to roll on its side. Alexander's eyes grew big as he saw that the body was naked. He got such a shock that he let go of the hand and the body surged back displacing filthy water which slopped over the boy's shoes.

Alexander rushed back home, tearing round to the back door he dashed into the kitchen. His father was just finishing his breakfast.

Both parents looked up as the door crashed back against the frame. Mouths opened to remonstrate, but Alexander beat them to it.

"I found a dead woman. She's been murdered … she's naked … and, guess what? I've seen her ..."

"Alexander!" shouted the boy's parents in unison. Gerald got up and grabbed his son's collar, while Elise stood transfixed with her hand to her mouth.

"Now, listen here, son," Jerry spoke quietly, but his son knew that it was the voice that brooked no nonsense, "quieten down; tell us exactly what you're talking about and, if this is another of your stories, I'll get the strap ..."

"No, Gerald. No!" Elise intervened quickly. "I'm sure Alexander wouldn't make up anything like that," She looked fondly at her son and smoothing back his hair, spoke in a soft soothing voice. "Tell me, dear,"

Now Alexander had the audience he wanted, he really let go, describing in minute detail what he saw; even pretending to be near fainting with terror, at the memory. "And, Dad, Mum," he concluded, "you must get the police, I'll go and stand guard near the body; no one must touch it – you know that from the movies – the police always say you must leave the crime scene alone," He went to go out the door, but his father grabbed him again.

"Elise, you go to the phone, ring the police and tell them about the body in the trough. Tell them where the trough is – in front of the Feed and Grain store. Ask them to send someone immediately. Also tell them that our son found the body, *accidentally*, and that I'm watching to see that no one touches it."

Jerry reached out and patted his wife. "You can do it, Elise. Now, off you go. I'll go with Alex and wait near the trough. The kid's right about not touching anything," He reached for his overcoat; the wind outside was piercing.

Elise began to tremble. Telephoning the police! No one in their previous area would have anything to do with the police but, here, she knew the 'nobs' were all in with them – while the people in the Quarry area, were exactly the opposite.

She straightened up; she would do her duty and be seen as a woman who knew the right thing to do and *how* to do it; but she must remember how to speak. The police were *not* gentlemen, so it would be right to speak haughtily – as befits their station.

Keeping that in mind, Elise went slowly into Gerald's study and picked up the phone.

Gerald and Alex went to the Feed and Grain store where Jerry saw the body for the first time. There had been another movement of the water, probably caused by Alex's wild pulling of the hand; the face was now clear.

Jerry Seymour took one look at the young woman's face and his own face turned a pasty white. "Bloody Hell!" he gasped. "It's *Jean*! Who's put her *here*? Now the fat's in the fire!" He thrust his son away from him, suddenly aware that the bloody kid had heard him call the girl by name.

NINE

"Is that the police? Yes, thank you. This is Mrs Gerald Seymour of Stone Cottage, Bexford North. I wish to report … a body … um … a death … a … um …er … a murder."

The voice on the other end of the line was calm and surprisingly courteous.

"Yes, madam and where would this body actually be? Is it at your own place?"

Mrs Seymour was incensed. She forgot all her resolutions. "Waddya mean? At my place? As if I'd 'ave a filthy body in my 'ouse. I'll 'ave y'know this is a respectable 'ouse, this is …" she was interrupted by the suave voice of the policeman.

"Would you please tell me, madam – if you are capable of coherent speech – just exactly where the body is that has been murdered, that is, of course, *if* there is a body at all?"

Elise actually screeched. "How dare you!" Then, with a tremendous effort, she lowered her voice, dragging her accent back in place. "I'll report you for your insolence. The body is in the water-trough in front of the Feed and Grain store in Sheridan Lane. My son, Alexander Montague Seymour, accidentally found the body, while my husband – who is an important and powerful man in a prominent Government Department – is guarding it at this moment,"

The calm voice answered. "Thank you, madam for your information. Inspector Peters will be there with his team directly. Good morning," The line went dead.

Mrs Seymour returned to her kitchen, unhappily aware that she had not shone in that exchange.

TEN

Telephone call from Mrs Annie Watson to her daughter, Penelope, now Mrs George McKenzie Jnr.:

"Penelope, darling girl of mine, it's only your old mother! It's good that you're up and about so early, but are you sure it's good for my granddaughter to be prancing around at this hour? … What? Oh course, I know you're only three months pregnant, but I want to make sure that the girl has a healthy start in life … How do I know it's going to be a girl? … Of *course* it is going to be a girl! I've already picked out the name, Ethelberta … Really! Penelope since you became a married woman you have become extremely coarse!

"Now, listen dearest child … to be serious for a change, I have something important to announce to you … are you ready? You are? Good. Now, when the baby is born, I demand to be called, 'Grannie Annie' … Stop laughing, I'm serious. I'm telling everyone here in the village that that's the only name I'll answer to, when the time comes around … Ssh! Quiet! And, another thing, I've told your father he is to be called, 'Grumpy Pumpy' … Well, to tell the truth, Penelope, I was surprised …you're right; he wasn't terribly thrilled by the name – I thought he'd love it. We could settle for 'Grumpy Pappy' if that makes him feel better.

"Now the important things are out of the way, the reason I rang you was to congratulate young George on his promotion to Chief Prosecutor for the Crown. I can't pretend to understand how all this works, dear, but I think I've got it right: There were a number of bright young men eligible but your George was chosen as the most competent of the whole lot. And, he'll lead the Prosecution in this very difficult and dangerous trial of a terrible gangster. Is that right?

"Thank heavens! I feel so proud of him. But I was a bit worried, dear, when he stopped being a defence lawyer and went over to the Prosecution... Why? It's perfectly simple, dear. I always thought I'd most probably end up needing a barrister one day to rescue me, from doing a stint in a uniform with arrows printed on it, so it *was* comforting to know we had a defence barrister in the family ... However, I *do* realise it's a tremendous promotion, love, so give George a big kiss from us ... What? You're having a special 'do' on Friday at Chambers to celebrate? Oh, goody! There'll be wonderful things to eat there ...

"What nonsense! Don't tell anyone you can't eat anything ...just take a bag with you in your biggest purse and bring all the good things home, then you can share out the lolly with us peasants here in the *boondocks* ... Well, I don't know what they are either dear, but the Americans here keep talking about 'being stuck out in the boondocks'. I thought I'd just throw it in the conversation to make it sound as if I knew what the hell they're talking about ...

"Oh, Penny! Wait a minute, I've just looked out the window. Inspector Peters and a group of police and villagers are grouped together in front of the Feed and Grain store. The ambulance is there as well. Dear God! I wonder what's wrong. ... What? Oh course not, it's nothing to do with me ... I've finished with crime, I've told you that before ...No, never again ... Oh, I'm sorry, dear Penelope, I've got to go ...

"Inspector Peters is making his way across here ... Well ... I'll *try*, Penny, I don't really want to be involved in any more ... Truly I don't ... well, *almost* truly ... Penny! That was rude! Speak to you later, love. Bye,"

ELEVEN

Bianca Firelli lifted the last awkward crate of flowers with the aid of her two sisters, Maria and Lucia, into the Nursery Cooperative lorry. It would transport the flowers to the markets. The three girls had picked for two hours, then spent an hour, tying the flowers into bunches. They were now weary and longing for breakfast. Their mother, Adela Firelli, would have it ready the moment they had finished.

"Listen," Bianca spoke hurriedly as they turned away from the lorry, "I'm just going to run up and see Dan for a moment. Tell Mum I'll be in for breakfast in about ten minutes," The two younger girls looked at each other and smiled, then hurried off to the house.

Bianca did run to the Kelly dairy. What a stupid thing to have done, she kept saying to herself. As if he didn't have enough to cope with as it is and for me to carry on like that! Mum says all girls are stupid and she's right. I certainly am.

As the farms were near each other, separated by paddocks, it only took a few minutes for the young Italian girl to cover the distance to the Kelly house. As she neared the building, she saw Dan storm out of the house and feared the worst – he was still angry.

She slowed her pace and was near to returning the way she had come, hoping he would not see her, when she heard him calling her urgently. She went on to him and quickly realised that it was obviously not her, he was upset about, it was something else. He held his arms open and she rushed into them – as into a safe harbour.

"Dan, what is it? Tell me darling; what has happened?" A sudden thought struck her and she grasped Dan tightly by the arms. "Dan," she whispered, "there hasn't been another telegram, has there?"

"Huh? No, thank God, nothing like that. If there's another one I think Mum will have a stroke!" Dan kissed his fiancé tenderly. "No, darling, it's that bloody Jean. She's gone missing – been out all night; bed's not been slept in."

"What!"

"And," Dan went on, "if that's not enough, there was a terrible scene at the breakfast table and fat Sally informed us she's leaving today as well. She can't stand us for a moment longer."

"Oh! Dan! What will you do? You and Hannah can't do it all! I wonder if one of us could be spared …"

"No, Bianca, that's out of the question. You and your mother and sisters are doing the work of four men – as well as your own; there's no way you can do more than what you're doing,"

Bianca knew he was right. With her father and three brothers interned, they were working under intense pressures, just to keep the business going.

"But, what will you do?"

"Listen, don't worry. We're getting on to the Milk Inspector and the Army authorities today. They'll just have to send us some help, and that's that. We're been suckers long enough – putting up with this situation, while others are just sitting on their arses doing nothing,"

Dan started to smile. "But I have to tell you that Sally said she wouldn't be in your place for a million quid, as you were marrying a toad with no sex appeal at all. There! So now you know what you're in for!"

"Would you think less of me, Dan dear," Bianca asked sweetly, her beautiful dark eyes flashing; "if she left your house, with a couple of black eyes? I've developed a pretty strong arm in the last couple of years! The nerve of her!"

Bianca's lips started to twitch. "Oh course, it's true in a way. I realise that you don't find me attractive in that way … Stop it, Dan! Stop it at once!" laughing, Bianca pulled away and kept a safe distance. They were standing at arms length, holding hands and happily devouring each other with their eyes, when they were brought down to earth by the strong voice of Hannah shouting from the open window.

"Dan, Dan! Come quickly. You, too Bianca! The police rang. They've found the wretched girl. Believe it or not … she's dead … she's been murdered!"

Dan felt suddenly as if he were going to be ill; he and his fiancé looked at each other. "Bianca, what will we do now? She's been found dead."

"Oh, dear God – and after what happened last night!"

TWELVE

Inspector Bob Peters shook his head wearily and smiled at Annie. They were old friends and had been colleagues in so many village tragedies. Peters was in his fifties; a neat, tidy, compact man, with regular features and grey hair.

He thought Annie Watson was one of the most singularly beautiful, and intelligent women, he had ever known; not beautiful in the conventual, or, fashionable manner, but in the wonderful bone structure of her face and the brilliant blue clearness of her startling eyes. He was always amused at her inability to manage her unwieldy crop of magnificent dark hair, which, he noted sadly was now showing vivid streaks of grey.

"Here we go again, Mrs Watson. It seems as if Bexford North is going to be in for yet another horror," Apart from his usual grey suit and conservative tie, Peters was obviously feeling the cold, as he was wearing an overcoat of a dark colour.

Annie noted sadly that the inspector, after all these years of war, with endless work and worry, was looking his age; his face was lined with fatigue.

"But what's actually happened, Inspector? I'm in the dark,' Annie replied.

"It's pretty terrible, I'm afraid," Peters answered. 'But, it's definitely murder, and the girl is most definitely local ..."

"Local? Dear God! Who is it?"

"It's one of the Land Army Girls; she worked for Mrs Kelly at the dairy. Her name is Jean Harris,"

"Oh, merciful heavens! What will Hannah do now?" Annie then realised what she had said. "God forgive me, that sounded as if I didn't care about the poor young girl being murdered.

"Oh course I do, but you know the score up there, Inspector. You know the struggle Hannah and Dan are having just trying to keep going and now, with one of the girls gone, what on earth will they do?" Annie grabbed Peters' arm. "Do they know yet, up at the farm, that it *is* Jean?"

"They do, Mrs Watson. I had to phone Mrs Kelly as soon as a couple of the men recognized the girl. Mrs Kelly informed me the girl had gone missing last night and had not returned home from going to the pub – or, at least that's where she told Mrs Kelly, she was going.

"Mrs Watson," the Inspector went on, "you are a good friend and confidante of Mrs Kelly, so I want to ask you to do two things: firstly, would you please take a look at the dead girl – it's fairly dreadful – and then to tell me if you know any gossip about her,"

"Oh course, I'll go and look at the poor girl. Do you know, I saw her last night … no … that's ridiculous, I couldn't have *seen* her – it was pitch dark with the blackout – but, I *did hear* her last night at half past nine o'clock, when I came out to close the front gates, Jean was arguing loudly with …um …er … a man …" Annie suddenly had a mysterious bout of coughing. She had been about to reveal the man's name, then stopped. Peter's noted the hesitation and thought it wise not to pursue that reluctance…for the moment.

Annie rushed on, hoping the inspector hadn't noticed her slip. "What a tragedy to see another young life cut short. She must be only about twenty-one or two,"

Annie grabbed an old sweater, as she was talking, pulling it on over her working clothes; she had been about to go out to the vegetable garden, so had men's thick boots on her feet, of which she was totally unaware. Peters filled in the details of the dead girl as they walked towards the Feed and Grain store.

"She's twenty-two, unmarried, has three siblings and her parents have rung me twice from Newcastle. Apparently they are furious that such a thing could have happened and seem ready to blame just about everybody."

"Oh dear, this is going to be hard on Hannah and Dan."

"Yes, I'm afraid it is. In the conversation on the phone I had with Mr Harris, he intimated that we need look no further than Dan, to find the murderer …"

"He didn't!" exploded Annie. "The cheek of him! I hope you gave him a piece of your mind."

Peters smiled.

"It's not quite as easy as that for me, Mrs Watson. Rarely, can I ever say what I really think, about anything. But I assured him that Mr Daniel Kelly would be kept in the picture, along with every other person – especially the men – until they are proven innocent."

Annie grimaced. "I'd never make the Diplomatic Corp, Inspector. But why would they immediately think the murderer is poor Dan? Is it just because he lived in the same house as the dead girl?"

The Inspector pulled at his ear with some agitation. "Well, not exactly, Mrs Watson, it seems as if Jean said something about being afraid of Dan, in her letters home to her parents."

"But, dear God! That could be easily explained. The girl, from what Hannah has said, was the laziest creature she has ever known; that she had proven useless in every task she had been given and both she and Dan had to watch her like a hawk, whenever she was doing anything – even the simplest tasks."

The inspector nodded as they crossed the road, then walked with Annie to the water-trough. The police, the local doctor and the ambulance men moved away and Annie saw the body for the first time. She gasped at the horrible sight, turning her head away quickly in horror, then with an impatient shake of her head, forced herself to turn back and study the dead girl closely.

"Are you all right, Annie," Dr Kemp asked, putting his hand on her arm.

"Yes, Edward," Annie answered. "I'm just being silly.

"Occasionally, I come over all feminine and womanly and have an attack of the vapours – it confuses dear Sam greatly – he's used to the rough and ready tough woman he married! Seriously though … dear God, we've seen enough dead bodies by now, in our little village, haven't we? But you never get used to it, do you? I don't know how you cope with it. Your good wife, Thelma, most probably has a lot to put up with."

Annie smiled at her friend and neighbour, then deliberately forced herself to take the hand of the dead girl; she then spoke to the Inspector.

"She is quite beautiful," Annie murmured, "slim, beautiful hair, delicate colouring. Her hands are lovely – how on earth did she manage that, working on a *farm*? Mine are a disgrace … I suppose you noticed the bruises on the wrists? Yes, of course you would. Are there any on the ankles? Yes? Well, that makes sense at any rate. Perhaps two people involved, do you think?"

The inspector answered. "Possibly, but not necessarily. One person could have used the wrists to push her in the muck, then held the ankles to pull her head under, and keep it under." Annie shivered suddenly, dropping the hand quickly.

"Inspector, there is such hatred and violence, in this death! It's a horrible death! Who could have hated this poor young girl to such an extent? It is undoubtedly a *passionate* crime; if you want to remove someone, there is no need to do so, in such a filthy and revolting manner. No, there is violence here; violence based on *hate* …

"Would there be much noise? Would she scream?" Annie wondered, and quickly corrected herself: "No, don't answer that. I do know that if a person is drowning, there is rarely any chance to scream; you are too busy trying desperately to breathe … so it could have been a very quiet, sinister affair … I see."

"And," added Peters, "with the total blackout, this trough, hidden as it is by the end wall, would be in total darkness – the perfect spot for a murder." Annie shuddered and moved away from the trough, to let the men get on with their work.

The ambulance men lifted the body from the water, placing it on a trolley, put it inside the vehicle as quickly as they could. The doors closed and it drove away.

The idle spectators drifted away, but Gerald and his son, Alexander, remained – they were talking to Sergeant Pierce, reluctantly on Gerald's part, with great delight on Alexander's.

Annie looked at Peters. "Do you need me anymore, Inspector? I would like to get up to see Hannah as soon as I can and I also have a casserole on the stove."

"I understand. Mrs Kelly would be very happy to have you with her now, I know. Just before you go, can you tell me anything else you have heard about the girl that would give us a lead?"

Annie lowered her head, trying to remember what Hannah had said about this particular girl. Something about nails … yes, that was it.

"Well, I know that Hannah said many times that Jean was lazy as sin, and spent her time fussing with her wretched nails, which she painted scarlet red. I did not really know the girl at all, Inspector. I only spoke to her a couple of times, in all the months she's been living here.

"Please God it may not be true, but, from the local gossip, I think it is possible that she was, what we used to call, 'man-mad'. I know she went to the pub most nights, if that helps. Tim and Betty Johnson, at the Inn, would know much more about her – they'd see her most nights."

Peters thanked Annie, and moved towards Gerald Seymour and

his son. Annie nodded to her new neighbour and smiled at Sergeant Piece, a particular friend of hers.

She wondered where Constable Potts was. It was unusual for him not to be with the inspector. She determined to ask about him as soon as the opportunity arose.

However, right now, she was determined to have her say to the Munroe brothers – the silly old chaps – about leaving the water-trough in that condition. And, she decided, this time she would not mince her words either – it was an absolute disgrace; they were not going to get away with their negligence.

But, first, she had to turn off the damn stove at home or the meat would be ruined. After that she'd tidy the kitchen and then she'd deal with the Munroe brothers – she was not her mother's daughter for nothing!

THIRTEEN

Charlie and Eric Munroe were working at the back of the huge Feed and Grain store when the elder brother saw who their new customer was. He hurried forward, his long old-fashioned apron reaching nearly to his ankles, but dressed as usual in his sober waistcoat and tie, with a winged starched collar. His brother, Eric, dressed exactly the same as Charlie, smiled and waved to Annie, before hurrying into the office at the rear of the building with parcels he was carrying.

"Miss Anne," Charlie greeted Annie. Annie always found it touching that these two old friends always thought of her as the daughter of the beloved Lady Mary and Sir Joseph Sheridan, whose ancestors founded the village of Bexford North so long ago.

It amused her to know that they found it hard to believe she was a middle-aged, married woman, with grown up children. "This is an honour. How can we help you?"

"Now, Charlie, you're not getting away with it this time, so don't even try."

"Get away with something, Miss Anne? I don't understand. Is something wrong? Something that I should know about?"

Annie looked at the elderly man. Could it be possible that he was unaware that a young woman was done to death in his water-trough, outside his store? No, it couldn't be; she was sure of that.

"You've had the police here this morning, haven't you?" The old man shuddered with distaste.

"Please lower your voice, Miss Anne," Charlie practically whispered. "For the first time in the history of the old place – police in here asking questions! Oh, poor father will turn in his grave. Oh, the scandal of it! What could be worse?"

"Well, Charlie," Annie answered calmly, "if it turns out that you or Eric actually murdered the poor young girl, then that would be worse." Charlie actually recoiled in horror.

"Miss Anne, I implore you …" the old man bleated.

"No, I'll have no pity on you Charlie Munroe. You and Eric have neglected your duties; you've let that old water-trough get so filthy; it's a disgrace to the village, the store itself and to your great father. You should be utterly ashamed of yourselves."

Charlie began to wring his hands. "I know, I know, you're completely correct, Miss Anne. It's our fault; it's our trough, but with those dirty men, coming from the pub …" he paused delicately.

"Yes, I understand that part of it. Perhaps a sensible thing would be to clean it out and put a hole in the bottom of it, so that everything would drain out; it would at least save it from becoming stagnant and filthy."

"Trust you, Miss Anne to have a sensible solution to the problem. We'll get on to it as soon as the police let us know that they are finished with it."

Annie tried another tack; it just might indicate another possible angle; the two brothers might have heard something about the dead girl.

"All right, forget the damn trough. Tell me Charlie, did you or your brother, know the girl Jean Harris at all?" To this innocent question, Annie was surprised to see Charlie's face begin to turn a bright red.

"Miss Anne, Miss Anne," he pleaded, "please lower your voice." The tall elderly man leant down to be even closer to Annie. "Please help me, I was so worried. Young Eric was simply infatuated with her; I actually found him *alone* talking with that young woman; I was so scandalised!"

Annie's mouth fell open in her surprise, until she realised how rude it would seem and shut it with a loud snap. Good God! 'Young' Eric had to be close to seventy – or more! She never really dreamt that he or Charlie would even know the girl. She hastily pulled herself together.

"I see, yes that makes it difficult for you, Charlie. I can see you've had a lot of trouble. Forget what I said about the trough; you've had your hands full with your own problems. Tell me, did Jean come to the store much?"

"Good God, *here*? No!" Charlie whispered, horrified at the suggestion. "But I once saw him go to the pub – neither of us ever done that before. Father did not permit any alcohol in our home – but one of the farmers told me Eric had actually spoken to that brazen young woman there. Please don't tell anyone. I was so embarrassed by this liaison. Father would have been ashamed of his son's behaviour." He lowered his voice even further. "I don't have to tell you, Miss Anne, that it's wrong to speak evil of the dead, but I think that young woman … was … a … a… *hussy*! There!"

The old man in his starched collar stood up straight and closed his eyes – the picture of outraged humiliation.

Annie was filled with a conflicting desire to burst out laughing and flush with embarrassment, at the same time. The thought of Eric the Philanderer, at his age, conducting an affair with the flashy young woman was comical, but she understood how horrendous this would seem to Charlie. She patted the old man's hand, and said softly.

"Well, Charlie, you've certainly had your share of worry, I can see that." Annie then whispered to Charlie. "Would it help if I spoke to Eric? He must be upset by her death. You know I wouldn't make fun of him."

Charlie took Annie's hand; he was touched by her kindness. "Thank you, Miss Anne that is so typically kind of you. However, thank heavens, there's no need, it was all over in a couple of weeks – it was just an old man being foolish."

Annie tried to think of a way to get out of this embarrassing conversation and, fortunately, spied a large new container of radiator anti-freeze. This was new; they had never stocked that before.

"Charlie," Annie asked, going to the shelf. "Is this stuff expensive? Sam is having trouble starting the car these freezing winter mornings. We've never used anti-freeze before. Does it work? I think the army vehicles use it, don't they?"

Charlie, with his mind now diverted from his family scandal, went into his sales pitch regarding anti-freeze. He was convincing, informing her that most of the locals who still had cars – and coupons to buy the precious petrol – had bought some from him and were delighted with the result. Annie decided to buy a pint of the liquid, but having nothing to put it in, Charlie rushed around until he found an empty soft drink bottle and filled it up for her. He then found a cork to fit the bottle.

Annie thanked him and went to leave the store, when he called her back. "I'm sorry, Miss Anne, I forgot to put this label on the bottle – it's a legal requirement. Just wait a moment!" So saying, he slapped a label with the word 'Poison' and a sketch of a skull and crossbones on the front of the bottle.

"Good gracious," exclaimed Annie. "Is it dangerous?"

"It's deadly, Miss Anne," Charlie answered, "not only to humans but to dogs and cats as well. It is ethylene glycol, so keep it up high up on a shelf in your garage, and tell your husband about it. But, he'll be delighted to see what it does to help start the car in the mornings – the directions are on the label I put on … No, never a trouble … thank you Miss Anne." Charlie hurried away to deal with a farmer who was tapping on the back counter impatiently.

Annie walked slowly back to her house carrying her bottle of poison, smiling as she thought of her old friend, Eric – dear, kind old man that he actually was. She thought again of the truth that, under the veil of respectability that enshrouded the village and with all their preoccupations concentrating on the war, there lurked endless other mysteries, secret longings and, equally secret, heart ache.

FOURTEEN

Previously, while Annie Watson returned home to attend to her kitchen after viewing the body and before she returned to tackle Charlie Munroe over the condition of the water trough, Inspector Peters had hurried over to Sergeant Pierce, who was still with Gerald Seymour and his son.

"Good morning Mr Seymour," Peters said, holding out his hand. "I'm Inspector Peters and I'm sorry you've had to stand around all this time in this bitter wind," The two men shook hands.

"No problem, Inspector," Gerald replied. "I'm warm enough with this coat and I don't have to be at work today, but Alex here has to be off to school, as soon as you can let him go." Alexander looked with dislike at his father; he now had no intention of hurrying off if he could help it; there were still exciting things happening here.

"And you work, where exactly, Mr Seymour? I see you have a car – you're a lucky man these days."

"At the Ministry of Agriculture, Inspector. I'm an economist; my job is allocating the Government funds to the farmers who grow our food – at least I'm one of a dozen or so, of the chaps, who decide that. I also am responsible for sitting on the Commission for the inspection and supervision of farmers, who are not utilising their land properly, in this time of war. I use the car, as I travel a lot."

"Yes, I understand you would. You have an important and difficult job," commented Peters. "Well, what can you tell me about this situation? Any information at all would be valuable. Did you know the young woman …" Alexander quickly interrupted, before his father could speak.

"Yes, Dad knew the girl. When he saw her he whistled and said: 'Blimey, that's Jean; the fat's in the fire now.'"

Gerald swung round to face his son and raised his hand in fury. Realising he was with the police, he pretended to use it to smooth back his rather long, blond hair. He tried to turn his son's bombshell into a joke.

"These young nippers, eh, Inspector? The bloody limit, aren't they?" He turned to his son. "Alex, what I said, meant nothing. Of course, I knew the girl, everyone did."

He turned to the Inspector. "As she was a constant visitor to the old pub, Inspector, I think just about everyone in this little village knew Jean. She had …," he raised his eyebrows, winking at the policeman, "quite a reputation. Thank the Lord I'm a happily married man. However, there will be quite a number of men in the area who will be unhappy that Jean was the victim."

Gerald was uneasy; he felt the need to extricate himself from what could be a potentially dangerous situation. He went on. "Oh course, I know it's not fashionable today to be religious, but as the Reverend Mr Norman says – we go as a family, to Church here, each Sunday – you can cheat people, but in the end you can't cheat God."

Peters looked at this tall, good looking man with increasing distaste. What age would he be, he wondered, thirty-five, thirty-six? Dresses well, expensive clothes, and the job obviously pays well; has a good car, bought Amelia's beautiful cottage outright – paid cash – or, so he had been told; does not seem to be effected by poor food. But … he's … what? Not a fool … no, a 'cad'; yes, he decided; that old fashioned word suited this chap well; that's what he reminds me of … a cad. Peters had met quite a number of 'Geralds' in his career.

Bob Peters put on his bland look, made some comments about Mr Seymour's remarks doing him credit, told him that's all he wanted – at the moment – and suggested Alexander could be getting on to school.

He shook hands again and he and Pierce slowly walked away, heads together, towards the Sheridan Inn, or pub, as it was generally called. Gerald looked a little disconcerted at being suddenly left, swore softly, and turned to his son.

"And, listen, you," he threatened, "just keep your mouth shut, when the police ask you anything at all. I forbid you to speak to them alone; they can't question you without your mother or me being there, remember that! If you mention again, *to anyone at all*, that I said I knew Jean – which I didn't – I'll take the strap from behind the bathroom door, and you'll feel it around those ugly legs of yours. Is that clear?"

Alex cowered before his father's fury. "Yes, Dad," he whispered, "I didn't think it was wrong. I won't say another word to them."

"You'd better not, or, you're in for a nasty surprise. Now, off you go to school and I hope you get the cane for being late."

Alex ran out of the lane and picked up his school bag from where he had dropped it inside the fence. He was excited: fancy, his Dad was probably the murderer! Wait till I tell the kids that! He might be hanged! Oh, I hope I'll be allowed to watch! He visualised the scene gloatingly in his mind.

With his head filled with bodies hanging from gibbets, Alexander was just about to walk towards the bus stop, when he paused. He had noticed the Watson woman going in the door of the Feed store – she was probably going to talk about the murder; that could be interesting.

Alex made a sudden decision; he would skip school; it could be much more fun to stay here and keep an eye on whatever the people, as well as the police, were doing. He cast a quick look around, then seeing the coast was clear, slipped silently through the open loading dock of the Feed and Grain store and, once in, hid behind a huge pile of bags of feed and bales of hay. He squirmed himself into a comfortable position, then climbed the bales until he reached a spot where he could not only see the counter, but could hear what was being said.

To his delight he was in time to see the woman with the 'toffy' voice from across the street, telling off the old goat, who owned the store. Alex listened, his eyes growing big, to the revelation of Eric Munroe knowing the dead girl! Alexander fumbled in his school bag and found a notebook and a grubby pencil.

This was important; it was necessary to get it all down; yes, definitely more interesting than school; there could be real money in this.

FIFTEEN

"What did you think of Gerald Seymour, Pierce?" asked Peters in a particularly dry voice, keeping his face deadpan; an expression which his Sergeant recognized immediately.

"Exactly what you did, sir," he answered, smiling. "A flashy, good-looking bloke, in a cushy job, possibly 'on the fiddle' and, as well as all that, I think it's highly probable he's very keen on the girls."

"You're a cynic, Pierce," Peters remarked. "After all, you heard him protesting about his God-fearing life, quoting the good Mr Norman and all."

"It'd be interesting to hear Mr Norman's opinion, on that," Pierce replied. "He's no fool; no hypocrite either. Mr Norman must have had dealings with the chap in the selling of the house; it was left to the minister, don't forget."

"That's right, Pierce," Peters admitted. "I had forgotten dear old Miss Tatley left it to Herbert Norman. We'll keep that in mind, if we need another opinion of our Gerald." Peters looked quizzically at Pierce. "So, we're agreed, Sergeant, a possible suspect?"

"Most definitely, sir; possibly aided by his revolting kid – the precious Alexander!" Pierce shuddered as a blast of cold wind caught his coat and blew it open. "Sir," he pleaded, "could we get out of this wind? We won't catch the murderer if we both catch pneumonia instead."

Peters laughed; together they entered the old Sheridan Inn where Tim Johnson, the publican, was waiting to receive them.

SIXTEEN

The elderly Constable Potts had had a busy morning. The inspector had sent him first of all to the Kelly farm, mainly as a visit of assurance that the 'team' were on the job and, with one of the Land Army girls dead, that they were also aware of the situation the farm was now facing, in regard to workers.

Hannah, as per usual, had insisted on giving Potts several cups of strong tea and some scones which she had been baking as soon as breakfast was over. Baking scones, for Hannah, was the perfect remedy, for nearly every disaster, or bout of anxiety and depression.

Fortified by Hannah's ministrations, Potts had gone on in the car to the large Military General Hospital which was situated at Wembley Park. The inspector had, when he had discovered the identity of the murdered girl, contacted his friend, the Colonel, there; Potts was sent to see if the quest had been successful or not; he was to meet both Peters and Pierce at the pub when he had completed his mission.

The Hospital had now grown into a huge institution. With all the years of war the number of wounded Australian soldiers, being sent home, was staggering; existing Hospitals were bursting at the seams, large private mansions were requisitioned, while new hospitals were being hastily put together, to try to cope with the problem.

The grounds of the Hospital which still bore traces of the glorious parklands of the previous Wembley Estate, had several sheltered areas, so the convalescent soldiers were able to get out, even on a cold winter's day such as this.

In these protected areas they were sheltered from the wind; the sun was pleasant as they sat, played cards, read, or simply lay back in their chairs, grateful for the warmth and peace of the beautiful garden.

There were few soldiers in the entire Hospital who did not carry terrifying reminders of the war in their limbs, their bodies and, especially, in their minds.

Constable Potts had to wait until the Colonel, who was their main surgeon as well, had finished in the operating theatre. He was then admitted to the grey-haired, weary man who was still wearing his blood streaked gown, with his theatre cap pushed back on his head.

He shook hands with Potts, took him in to his office and offered him a shot of whisky, which the elderly policeman politely refused. Only then did the Colonel give Potts the answer to take to his superior officer.

Potts thanked the Colonel on the Inspector's behalf, gave the information the Colonel requested, then getting back in the car drove smartly off to meet his colleagues back at the pub.

SEVENTEEN

As the policemen entered the old Sheridan Inn they were immediately aware of a change in the decoration of the foyer. Over the front desk was a large, beautifully carved, wooden copy of the Sheridan crest, complete with its motto: 'Nolite timere, veritas vincit' – do not be afraid, Truth conquers.

"I wonder why they have reinstalled that," Peters murmured to Pierce.

The men were not kept long in suspense as Tim Johnson hurried out to meet them.

There were genuinely happy greetings, as the police knew Timothy Johnson very well indeed, from the time he had been a helpless, wounded soldier in the Convalescent Hospital in the village, which at the time of Major Johnson's illness, was called a Mental Hospital.

The police had formed strong friendships with some of the soldiers, at that place, as they worked on a series of baffling murders which had occurred there. Tim had been eventually medically discharged from the Army and had married another friend of the police, Betty Fletcher, the right-hand worker and assistant of the aged publican, Mr Joe Jones.

Both Joe and his dearly treasured wife, Biddy, now dead, had loved the girl and had regarded her as their own child and, to the girl's immense surprise, had willed the entire business to her. Betty now worked, with her husband, as the manager of the Inn.

"Once again, Inspector," Tim said, "you are very welcome. Betty sends her greetings; she'll be along soon. She was saying this morning, after the news got to the pub about Jean, that we only see you when there's some disaster or other."

"That's about it," agreed Peters. "I see you're got the Sheridan crest up here in the foyer. That surprised me, but I'm happy to see it; it goes with the name of the Inn which is a valuable historic building,"

"It is that, Inspector, but I'm afraid it's there for a very prosaic, practical reason," Tim smiled ruefully.

"You see, we've been having trouble with the licensing board about our closing times. It's never been a problem before, but now with the precious Mr Gerald Seymour – a kind of 'Inspector-General' – living here in the village, we've had to explain the exemption we have enjoyed to the usual six o'clock closing rule, for pubs."

"Do you know, Tim," Peters remarked, wonderingly, "in all the times I have been here, the fact that you closed later than other pubs, never occurred to me. What kind of copper does that make me?"

"And, that's weird really, for the wretched surveillance of closing times, is one of our biggest headaches – and the greatest waste of our precious time. But, now that you've brought it to our attention, how on earth do you get around the law?"

"Please excuse me for interrupting, sir," Sergeant Pierce added, smiling, "let me say before you start explaining, that I, for one, am very happy that you have been able to remain open. Dear old Mr Jones often came to our rescue in the past."

"It's a strange situation, gentlemen," Tim explained, smiling at Pierce's remark. "When old Sir Patrick Sheridan had this Inn built – and, remember he built an *Inn*, not a pub – he and the Governor of the time were as thick as thieves. Of course they would be – it stands to reason – Sir Patrick was extremely rich; he had built the mansion called the Big House and he had also established the village out here, in what was then thought of, as the back of beyond." Tim laughed.

"Anyhow, both Sir Patrick and the Governor, were anti the Temperance powers in politics and they, somehow or other, wrangled a Charter which for Inns, which provided accommodation, as well as liquid refreshments, to determine their own opening and closing times as long as …and I quote from the Charter: 'that in these country districts it does not interfere with the sober, Godly right-order of society, indicates publicly allegiance to the monarch gloriously reigning and which does not contribute to the growth of godlessness, unseemly or unbecoming behaviour, within the parish confines, in which it be located'. It also adds that 'under no circumstances, whatsoever, must alcoholic beverages be served during the sacred hours of six o'clock and midday on the Sabbath day'.

"So, if you didn't know it already, Inspector, you are now in the country, or the boondocks, as the Americans call it and different rules apply to us."

"That's a load of baloney, Tim, which you know full well – the law covers the whole of Australia." Peters, genuinely diverted, by the ridiculous so-called 'Charter', responded, laughing. "However, in our time here at Bexford North, we've never had one single case of drunkenness, or disorderly conduct, to have to deal with, so, believe me, we shall be quite happy to go along with your spurious 'Charter' for it suits us as well." The three men laughed companionably together.

"So that explains why the Sheridan crest has been resurrected and placed in such a prominent place in the foyer; as well as a portrait of His Majesty," Pierce commented. "Makes sense, really. Did you have a spare crest, or did you have one made?"

"Had it made," Tim explained. "There was a chap down at the Convalescent Hospital, well on the way to recovery, thank God, who'd been a wood carver in civilian life.

"I asked Major Waters – he still in charge down there, as the chief doctor – whether I could ask this chap to have a go at the crest.

Ted Waters thought it would be a good idea, so we got a beautifully carved, wooden crest – copied from the stone crest over the entry to the Big House down there – which looks authentically old, genuine …"

"And impresses the locals," finished Peters. "A very sensible thing to do." The Inspector turned to his Sergeant, "Right, that's that. Pierce we'd better get back to the murder which we're supposed to be investigating."

He looked back at Tim. "Could we go into the small parlour, Tim for a short talk? You realise how important your testimony is as I know the girl was here at the pub – excuse me … at the *Inn* – last night."

"I understand perfectly, Inspector." Tim nodded his agreement. "Come this way; I've lit a little fire in the parlour in case you were coming here, so it'll be warmer in there but the fire's a bit smoky. Later on, if you have time, Betty would love to give you a cup of tea, just say the word."

The policemen thanked their host and followed him into the small room which they knew so well. Peters thought Tim had been right about the fire – it was definitely smoky; anyhow it was much warmer than the other rooms. The men sat down and Sergeant Pierce took out his notebook.

Before they could begin, there was a hesitant knock on the door. It opened slightly and the elderly face of Constable Potts put his head around the door.

"Would you like me to join you, sir," he asked, "or, is there another job you want me to do?"

"No, come in, Constable. You need to hear Tim's answers and I want to know how you got on up at the Kellys and the Hospital."

Constable Potts greeted Tim Johnson happily, then settled himself to give his report. Peters turned to Tim.

"Do you mind just waiting a moment or two, Tim, until I hear what our good Potts has to tell us?"

"Of course not; it's always a pleasure to see Constable Potts anyway."

"Right, then, Potsy! Firstly: was the Colonel cooperative?"

"Indeed, yes, sir," Potts replied, checking his notes. "In all, he has ten men that are ex-farm hands and are among the convalescing soldiers. He understands, perfectly, the predicament the Kellys are in and is only too willing to help. He said it stands to reason that the Army should do something; they take all the milk."

"So?"

"So, sir, the Colonel thought that he would try four of the men – the fittest of the ten with farm backgrounds – this afternoon to see if two on, two off, one hour's milking at a time, would work for the men.

"He has to be careful that he doesn't knock them about, but he thought that four of them are well enough advanced to, at least give it a try, until new Land Army Girls are supplied. He's contacting Mrs Kelly about the experiment, this morning."

"That sounds great, Constable, thank you," Peters replied. "Did he give any indication that he would lend his support to Mrs Kelly's request for more Army girls?"

"Indeed he did, sir. He said he would get straight on to the Army bloke in charge of that section and would give him – to use his words, sir – give him such a blast that he'd think Hell had fallen in on him; he'd be in shock for a week." Potts' listeners laughed appreciatively.

"Well, that's some relief for that poor woman and her son. Right, we'll be seeing Mrs Kelly after we're finished here, Potts. Now, Tim, tell me what you know about the murdered girl."

Peters was interrupted again by the door opening and Betty, Tim's wife, came into the room. She advanced on the Inspector, then shook hands with all the men in turn. She turned her attention to the fire.

"Isn't that just like men?" she demanded. "Tim, how could you let the fire get like this; it might warm the police but they'll probably choke to death on the smoke. Really!"

Tim looked a bit shamefaced. "Sorry, love, forgot it. I'll try to fix it," He started to get up. Betty restrained him with her hand on his shoulder.

"Stay where you are. You men! You never think of the simplest things to fix anything. I'll just open the window a bit from the bottom; with this wind it'll soon clear the room," Betty had the window open a little in a trice, then smiling at the men, reminded them of morning tea coming up later, if they wanted it. She then left the room.

"I'm a lucky man, Inspector," Tim said proudly.

"You are indeed, Tim," Peters agreed heartily. "And well deserved after what you've been through. But," Peters added, raising his eyebrows, slightly, "is there, by any chance, another little Johnson on the way to the pub?"

Tim blushed scarlet. "I've been dying to tell you chaps ever since I found out myself. That's why Betty wasn't there to greet you, when you arrived. She's been as sick as a dog most mornings lately, but we're both so happy about the coming event."

The police congratulated the father-to-be, and then got down to the business of the murder.

EIGHTEEN

Telephone call from Annie Watson to Harriet McKenzie, her daughter's mother-in-law:

"Harriet? Annie here ... No, I'm disgustingly well, thank you, and you? That's good ... Harriet, I told Sam that now you and I are going to become grandmothers, I've decided two things: firstly that I want to be called, 'Grannie Annie', secondly, that I'm going to try my hardest to be refined and respectable and not mess with murders and mysteries, things like that ...

"What's that? You're laughing at me! The nerve! It's always your *oldest* friends – notice I stressed the adjective, Harriet – who hurt you the most.

"Seriously love, I know that Penny is thrilled to bits and acting as if no one in the entire world has ever had a baby before, but do you know how Young George is taking it? ... Deliriously happy? Oh, I'm so glad of that.

"Listen dear. I've been concerned about our new neighbours – the Perry and Seymour families – about how we can include them in our activities here. I know the Perrys bought the lovely old Nicholls' house, next door to you, while the Seymours, of course, bought our beloved Amelia Tatley's stone cottage – directly opposite me. ...

"Well, I'm wondering if you can think up any ideas. You know how lonely it can be when you come to an area where you know nobody; I'd like to help if I can. I dropped in for a few moments the other day, just to welcome Mrs Perry – a very nice lady indeed – and I thought the poor young woman looked at her wits' end; she was trying to unpack, and to look after her brood of kids. Four, isn't it? And all under six, God help her! I haven't met Mr Perry yet, have you? What did you think of him? … Really? Oh dear! …

"Well, we'll just have to wait and see; might improve as we get to know him better. Have you managed to see Mrs Perry yet? … Oh course, you would have. Tell me, what is her first name? She asked me to call her by it, but I can't remember it, so I settled for the 'um …ah …' approach. Do you know it?

"Oh, *Cassandra*, that's nice? I hope she doesn't! … What? … Oh, dear Harriet, naughty, naughty; you're forgetting your Shakespeare. Remember, dear, Cassandra was always bleating out doom and disaster from the castle walls of Troy … I hope she doesn't here; so embarrassing! It's lucky there isn't a castle near by …

"Well, I'm trying to be serious, Harriet; you know it's difficult for me – something wrong with my heredity, I think – but, anyhow, I've thought of a good idea, regarding our new neighbours – it probably isn't – but here goes:

"What about inviting the two new-comers to a meeting in the pub on Saturday morning? In that way the men could look after the kids for a change. We could gather all the available women and say that we want to see if we could change our Occupational Therapy activities down at the Convalescent Hospital – perhaps not *change* them, but increase the *variety*.

"It's not a fib, either. I know if I have to keep trying to teach the same dances over, and over, and over, I'll go nuttier than the poor chaps down there. What do you think? Oh that's good … you never want to see French knitting ever again? Oh, that's exaggerating, Harriet, forty thousand feet of French knitting! Surely not!

"However, dear, I do understand – you're sick to death of it!

Well, we'll have to think of new things to do. I think we should be adventurous – daring – try really risky things … I really don't know *what* though … Anyhow, you think the meeting is a good idea?

"Fine, I'll see Mrs Seymour – *her* first name is Elise. Harriet, I've heard on the grapevine that the family is *very* wealthy … yes …and you'll see Mrs Perry about the meeting? – Another wealthy family; our little village is becoming truly grand now – I don't know how they'll put up with the likes of me, however …

"Isn't it strange to think of a new *young* family living in Amelia Tatley's house, with another new *young* family in dear old Major Nicholls' house as well? Oh, well, we're the oldies in the village now, Harriet.

"Must go … poor Hannah's Land Army Girl being murdered has caused more grief up at the dairy …Yes, you're right there, simply dreadful … No, of course I shall not be interfering in the investigation, Harriet, how could you suggest such a thing! …

"Well …that's true, I *did* go with Inspector Peters to see the corpse this morning – yes, drowned in that filthy water-trough – what an awful way to die … Yes, it's definitely murder; there were bruises on her wrists and her ankles … No, that's the absolute end of my involvement … *Harriet*! That was a rude word, Harriet! Let's change the subject …

"Dearest Florrie! She must be very near her time I think, isn't she? She's mountainous, but looks great – positively glowing, isn't she? Please God, the delivery will go well. I think she and Stephen have a wonderful marriage; this baby will be such a blessing … Names?

"Well, I've always got a store of them. I offered suggestions to Florrie and Stephen: If it's a boy, then I thought, Egbert, Godofo, Oberon and Agamemnon; if it's a girl Petruccia, Clytemnestra, Juno and Euphemia. What do you think? … Strange, that's the same reaction that Stephen and Florence had.

"No more clowning … Saturday at the pub, dear, if we can arrange it … about ten? Bye, love to your George. Is he happy to be soon a grandfather? No? Neither is Sam – men don't like being reminded they're growing old either – despite their protestations to the contrary… Bye dear."

NINETEEN

Alexander Seymour stayed in the Feed and Grain store after the Watson woman had left the building. He listened to some dull conversations and was soon bored. He began to wonder where the police would be in the pub. He knew there was a small parlour there and thought that could be a likely place.

Alex realised if he could use the alley by the side of the pub wall; the window of the small parlour opened onto it. It would be quite safe, as no other houses overlooked the alley and it was rarely used. They might be somewhere else, but it was worth a try.

If he left the store now, he could slip out the back way to the pub, through the Oval, then around that way. Then he could creep into the alley from the back. Of course, if the police are not talking in there, or if the window is shut, then he'd have to think of something else.

If that was the case, he would scuttle back to the store; it was a wizard hiding place, and you never knew what kinds of information he might pick up there, until it was time for him to return home at the regular time he was expected.

TWENTY

Tim Johnson explained to the police that Jean Harris was a frequent visitor to the bar, after work finished up at the dairy.

"She was here at least three nights a week, sometimes more. The other nights, she told me she went to the Pictures, or to a Dance. I don't know how she managed to get up early in the morning for milking; she certainly didn't get to bed early."

"Could that be the reason why everyone seems to be talking about how lazy the girl was?" ventured Constable Potts, who as usual, was always ready to find an excuse for everyone.

"I'm sorry, Constable," responded Tim, "but I think she really was a lazy girl. She was out for a good time and didn't see why the war should prevent her from having it.

"She made it pretty clear she had no intention of ruining her hands by actually *working*. Why she ever volunteered for the *Land Army Girls* I'll never understand; she had no idea of what work on a farm was like.

"She flirted with every bloke in the pub and had a fairly lurid reputation among the men. I had to intervene on a couple of occasions, when she was being used in bar-room jokes." Tim shrugged his shoulders expressively. "I mean there are limits! This is a very respectable pub, where the majority of our customers – especially those from the village itself and the Quarry area – are decent men who have little time for filthy talk."

"But, Tim," shrewdly suggested Inspector Peters, "I imagine that your opinion of the usual customers of the pub, does not include the soldiers, who are permitted to come here from either of the two Hospitals?"

"No, you're right there. Although, it's rare that a soldier from the Convalescent Hospital is allowed out at night, or even to drink at all. Most of them, even the healthiest, are on rather strong medication of some sort; that usually restricts, or prohibits, the drinking of alcohol."

"But what about those from the General Military Hospital?" Peters asked. "Sergeant Pierce was up there the other day and he said a large contingent of the soldiers, who were well on the road to recovery, were on their way here for some drinks – with their superior, Colonel Carter's, full approval."

"That's right sir," Pierce added, "I agreed to pack as many as I could into the police car and drove them here myself, then went off home."

Tim looked embarrassed. "Yes … well, the soldiers from there are another story altogether. To complicate matters – as far as I'm concerned – we now have a number of American soldiers, being treated there as well. I have nothing against the Americans; I'm fully aware that they are saving our country, in the Pacific war, but I do wish they would stop bragging about their own country."

"What do you mean, sir," asked Pierce.

"It leads to fights, Sergeant, that's what I mean. Especially after they've had a few drinks. The Australian soldiers resent being told, again and again," Tim adopted an exaggerated American accent: 'they couldn't save their own country; that they had to have America come to their aid; that America is the greatest, biggest, wealthiest, fairest, God-given country in the entire world – in fact it *was* God's own country.'" Tim pulled a wry face and all the men chuckled.

"I can see the situations very clearly, Tim," Peters commented. "And I can easily imagine the Australians' answer to the Americans:

that they only come into a war when it is nearly over; that they were almost not there, in the First World War; they were only interested in this war, after their precious Pearl Harbour was attacked." He sighed. "I wonder we haven't been called out here frequently to intervene. It's a credit to *you* that you have kept order."

"It certainly is," Potts added.

"But," continued Peters, "about Jean. It seems to be an established fact that she was, what used to be called, a 'good time girl,' but was she particularly close to any man, or men, in particular?"

"That's difficult, Inspector," replied their host. "Jean was popular with virtually all the men, called them all by their first names, old and young; was lavish with her hugging, blowing kisses and such. But, particular ones ... let me think," Tim closed his eyes and then spoke slowly. "Yes, I'd have to say that she was pretty thick with ... Gerald Seymour ... Alan Darcy ... Ron Perry ... Toby Moore. She was also pretty close with a couple of the old chaps – strange but true. One of them was Bert Liveridge ..." the policemen groaned, in unison, at the name, "and I think there was some hanky-panky going on with old Alf Cookson."

"No! Not Alf!" exclaimed Constable Potts, shocked. "He's the very model of respectability; someone I thought we could rely on totally."

"Potts, old son," reprimanded Peters, "Alf is a man like all others. Jean was a very pretty young woman. Alf would be flattered if she gave him any attention, as would any old chap," He turned to Tim. "Thank you Tim, you've certainly given us a list to work with." He looked closely at the publican. "Tim, I think you're holding something back; protecting someone. Please tell us. You know us; we're not likely to hound the poor bloke, if we find he's in the clear."

"Well, I hate to say it because I like the man and admire him so much as well. But I have to say I think there could be something going on between Dan Kelly and Jean – in spite of all they allegedly said about each other."

There was silence in the room; the silence of embarrassed shock.

"But," objected Potts at last, in an outraged voice, "he's engaged to Bianca!"

"That's the problem. Last night they had a terrible argument here in the pub, and it was over Jean; I didn't hear much of it, except the last bit. Bianca stormed off saying something like: 'Get back to the pretty, long nailed bitch and don't come near me again,'"

Tim looked stricken with remorse at revealing the argument, so he hurried on to other names. "Then, there were the soldiers. She was mainly thick with the Yanks. There was a Mitch, a Spike, an Andy and a Baz – I don't know the surnames." Tim looked up. "That's about all I can recall."

"And it's quite enough, thank you," groaned Peters. "Lord, chaps, this makes it difficult. Oh, well, we should be used to it by now. So, it's off we go to hunt all these blokes up: where were they last night; how close were they to the victim; did they see her often; did they have an argument; did she threaten them in any way, etc. You know the drill." Peters stood up.

"But, just before we go, Tim, are you able to tell us three things: who did Jean speak to last night? What time did she leave the pub? And, did she leave with anyone?"

Tim shut his eyes tight. "Let me think for a moment, Inspector. Right! I think I remember her speaking to each of the men I have already mentioned; she left about a quarter past eight o'clock and no, she left the pub on her own – I'm sure of that. I think I was surprised, when she darted off. I suppose, if I thought of it at all, I thought she had a rendezvous lined up outside."

"Thank you Tim, that's very helpful. Apologize to Betty for us not staying to speak to her; hope to catch up later. And thank you again for giving us this room as our headquarters here in the village. We certainly appreciate it."

He turned to Pierce, "Before we leave the pub, Pierce, phone through to the station; we need Manders and Watkins here as quickly as they can make it – tell them to each come by car, we need two more men – we've got a powerful lot of people to try to see today; I want everybody back here in the pub between half past four o'clock and five o'clock this afternoon, for a briefing. Is that clear?" Sergeant Pierce nodded and hurried out, just as Betty was coming in; they nearly collided. Both apologized, and Betty came in with a platter of sandwiches.

"Inspector, I know from the other times you've had to use the pub here, as your headquarters, there's never enough time for you men to get something to eat, so I've made some sandwiches." Peters smiled at the pretty young woman.

"You're a good and understanding woman Betty Johnson, just like your good mother; by the way, I saw her the other day, still cooking down at the Convalescent Hospital. Believe me a copper is always grateful if he can get a meal, *somewhere* near the usual time other people do."

"You're welcome, Inspector," Betty replied. "You've helped us enough in the past, God knows."

Tim intervened. "But, Betty, the inspector was just about to leave; they're in a hurry."

"No problem. I'll just slip these into a paper bag and you can take them with you."

"Sensible as well as beautiful, your good wife, Tim," commented Peters. "You look after her properly, won't you?"

Betty blushed, and hurried from the room. Peters returned to the subject matter of the murder.

"Tim, we have to get this sorted out as quickly as we can. I never dreamt that there would be so many suspects. Ah well! What's new? In the last case here in the village, nearly everybody living here, was a suspect!"

Tim laughed and led the policemen out of the pub assuring them that the room would be at their disposal whenever they wanted it.

They thanked him and left, while outside the window, Alexander was writing furiously – the spelling atrocious – the list of names – he'd fix up the spelling later. He never dreamed he'd hear such a lot of exciting information. Already his mind was devising ways and means of turning all this into profit as he, quietly and secretly, made his way back to the store where he hid again, among the bags of feed.

When he was settled and comfortable, he opened his lunch box. He had not realised that detective work could make you so hungry.

Back at the pub, when Sergeant Pierce had completed his telephone calls, he joined the other two policemen as they sat in the Inspector's car. They needed privacy – and a place out of the wind – in order to eat their sandwiches. They also had to decide on their plan and division of labour, while they waited for the young constables to arrive from Tavistock police station – with the extra cars.

TWENTY-ONE

Sally Flinders sat miserably at her bedroom window at the dairy farm. After the flare-up at breakfast she was actually regretting what happened. In spite of the words she had used in anger, she believed Hannah and Dan were good people, who worked like slaves.

Sally was a worker – not like that dratted Jean; she admired men and women who actually worked – worked with their hands – as she did. However, she realised they would never forgive her for what she'd said, and *why* – she asked herself – why … had she said it? To support a worthless, fool of a girl who was so bloody lazy it was an effort for her to get out of bed in the morning and – as for her morals!

Sally was no prude, but she thought Jean was a promiscuous tart – nothing more.

The old woman, Hannah, was right about the precious Jean. And yet, the men flocked to her; Jean could have any man she wanted in the whole village. Sally was painfully aware that the men had awful names about *her*. She had heard men saying while she was within hearing distance, in the pub: "Where's the pretty one tonight? There's no one here except the fat cow."

Men were so rottenly cruel. Since Jean had really started on the men, Sally tended to stay, more and more frequently, at home at night; it was no fun sitting there watching her work-mate being the one who was cuddled, kissed and bought drinks, while she sat and smiled, as though she enjoyed the spectacle.

Sally looked at herself critically in the mirror. No, I'm not pretty, but I'm damn well not ugly, either. Yes, I'm overweight and I can't seem to get it off, but everyone can't be one of those bone-thin, skeleton, movie-star types you see on the Pictures. Ordinary girls are just like me – the pretty ones, are few and far between; it's all so rottenly unfair.

Sally had started going to the Pictures of a night, instead of the pub. Even though she went on her own; it was better than being in a group that didn't want you, except to poke fun at you.

Then, why the hell had she stood up for Jean this morning? She wasn't worth it. Why did she promise that slut not to tell about her going to meet that bloke! Why, why, why! It was stupid, yes, a stupid thing to do and now she'd done it!

As the die was cast and she had been ordered to leave, Sally wanted very badly to stay.

When she had packed all her things and was fighting back tears, there came a loud knock on her door. Hannah opened the door and came into the room. She had been intending to finish off what she had started this morning at breakfast, but Hannah was a com-passionate woman, rough in tongue, but, basically, a very fair and honest, woman – more used to rough sons, than young girls.

She looked closely at the young woman's face; at her overweight body, her chubby cheeks and red rimmed eyes, hesitated for a moment, then said abruptly, holding out her arms: "Come here, child."

Sally took one look at her boss, and rushed like a little child, into her mother's arms. Her sobs were heart-tearing and her tears were flooding Hannah's ample breast. When she could manage it, Sally tried desperately to apologize. Hannah stopped the flow.

"There, there," she soothed the distraught girl as though she were a highly nervous cow. "Look, let's start again, shall we? You were quite right about me: I am a loud-mouthed, rough woman and

I put my foot in my mouth most times I open it. I'm sorry lass for the things I said about you and I would truly be fearfully upset if you took me at my word and left us."

"But the Colonel from the Hospital is sending other milkers this afternoon, isn't he Mrs Kelly? You won't need me anymore. I'm truly sorry for what I said. I shouldn't have stood up for Jean – she basically wasn't worth it. And, to tell the truth, I've truly enjoyed working here with you and Dan."

"That's what I mean, lass, we'll start again. And you can start by calling me Hannah, instead of Mrs Kelly. Don't worry about the extra milkers; if I know anything about men, they'll soon get tired of the novelty and give up. But you'll be needed as never before while we've got the new blokes here; they'll need instructing all the time, and you know how we do everything now."

Sally started to look up, then to smile. Hannah gave her a little shake and, leaving the room, said over her shoulder: "Come into the kitchen, Sally and we'll have a cup of tea and you can tell me all you know about the dratted Jean – God have mercy on her poor wretched soul – the silly, silly, young girl."

To her own astonishment, Sally answered: "Amen,"

TWENTY-TWO

Telephone call from Mrs Penelope McKenzie to her mother, Annie Watson.

"Mum? Sorry to keep you from your work, but I'll only be a couple of minutes. I forgot to tell you something very important when you rang me earlier ... Well, it's your own fault, with your 'Grannie Annie' rigmarole and everything ... Anyhow, try not to distract me with any more of your nonsense, or I'll forget to tell you what I must.

"Remember you rang me to congratulate George on his promotion as Prosecutor for the Crown? ... Yes, well, he's just rung me to tell me something that's happened. It's important news, so pay attention, Mum. You may have heard of the gangster Al Fordham? ...Yes, that's the one; murders galore, every sort of sleaze ... A horrid, dreadful man. Anyhow, the police were finally able to get sufficient evidence to get a conviction ... Yes, it is great news; he's a monster ...

"Unfortunately, already there's trouble. You see, as soon as the newspapers revealed the trial will now continue with a new Prosecutor, then *named* the barrister, George has received death threats ...

"Mum? *Mum*? *MUM*! Are you still there? You haven't fainted, or anything, have you? ... Well ... I suppose, I should have been a bit slower in coming out with the shocking news ... Of *course*, George is not abandoning the case – the trial is well underway; it's a tremendous opportunity for him, but I want you to pray for him. I think I'll die if anything happens to him ...

"No, I'm absolutely determined not to cry, Mum ... No, I'll be of no use to George if I'm a weak, soppy person; he and I just have to cope with this situation ... Well, the threats came by phone actually, but the police have warned that George will most likely get more calls, as the case goes on. I'm sorry, Mum but I can't talk about it anymore.

"Let's change the subject quickly. Do you know, Mum, that the junior barrister assisting George is none other than a relative of ours? ...Who? ...Cousin Edwina's boy, Greg *Sheridan* ... I thought you'd be interested. I don't remember ever meeting Cousin Edwina, but I've heard you speak of her – from the fabulously wealthy, country, Sheridans aren't they?

"Edwina's husband, Dudley – is that his name? – has the title, hasn't he? Oh, he's Greg's father? ...the wretch didn't tell me ... An interesting coincidence: being in the same Chambers as George ... Yes, we've met; he's a very nice man and very proud of our family name; he spoke glowingly of you – probably doesn't know you well ...

"No, dear, I didn't really mean that ...Well, that's all the news. Try hard not to worry, just pray for us. Bye."

Annie bit her lips. *Try not to worry*, she thought, that's a tall order! Try not to worry with my very first granddaughter receiving death threats?

TWENTY-THREE

Telephone call from Mrs Harriet McKenzie to Annie Watson.
"Annie did you hear the dreadful news? I nearly fainted on the spot … That's exactly what I thought … I was worried as soon as he was asked to lead the Prosecution; he was much safer doing defence …

"Yes, it's a tremendous promotion but, Annie, *death threats*! That's my baby boy that, 'they' – whoever *they* are – are threatening to kill! I can hardly believe it … Annie, my own George is a wreck and, wouldn't you know, manlike, he's trying desperately not to show it; I think he'll go completely grey by the time this trial is over; God grant that it is soon …

"Well, apparently this gangster, Fordham, has accomplices everywhere … The police? Well, they have already assigned two constables to accompany Young George when he is in public; they also patrol near his house at night … Penny didn't tell you that?

"No … don't blame her, Annie; most probably trying not to worry you. It was my George who got that information from the police; it helps with him being a solicitor, they tend to tell him things … Yes, if you or I asked, they'd tell us to mind our own business – as if this *isn't* our business!

"I know Annie, that's exactly what I said to both, young and old George, and I know Annie, that you don't need reminding about praying for them … thank God for that … You're right, that's all we can do … Oh, dear, I think I'm going to cry – I'm a fool, as if *that* will help! … And, we've got that meeting at the pub tomorrow morning for the ladies; I hope I can be sensible, Annie, and not make a fool of myself …

"I'd better hang up now … Bye, dear."

TWENTY-FOUR

While waiting for the young constables, Inspector Peters was writing lists of names as he divided the duties for the day.

"Pierce, you take Watkins when he gets here and go to Wembley Hospital and see if you can find those four Americans whose names we have – Mitch, Spike, Andy and Baz. We only have the first names, but I don't think you'll have any difficulty finding them.

"We might have to bring them in for questioning, but we'll have to be careful there; we are treading on military jurisdiction, so we'll have to go softly, softly. Then, I want you to check out those two new families in Quarry Lane – the Darcy and the Moore families. I don't know if you can get all that done in what's left of the day, but the important thing is I want all those involved to know that we know about them."

Peters turned to Potts.

"Potsy, you take one of the cars; you have my total sympathy, but I want you to try out your grandfatherly charm on our old protagonist, Bert Liveridge and on his neighbour Alf Cookson. I think we will find that the two old chaps had nothing to do with the murder, but I want you to ask them, Potts, if the young woman made requests for money from them. I think the answer could be interesting."

Peters scratched his head. "They could easily have had their heads turned by a bit of flattery from that scheming young woman, but it's equally possible that they were engaged in something else altogether with her, other than philandering – I've got an idea running round in my head about those two fellows. Anyhow, Potts try to find out all you can."

"Do my best, sir," answered the Constable.

"Before I finish with you, Potts, I want to know *where* exactly in the Quarry Lane are the new families, the Darcys and the Moores."

"As far as I know, sir, the Darcy family has taken that empty cottage, at the beginning of the Lane and the Moore family, is in the very last cottage. That end cottage was where old Miss Wilson lived; she died two months ago; used to be maid up at the Wembley Estate; was a sad end, she wasn't found for three days. She was ninety-three when she died."

"Indeed! Remarkable age!" Peters read again from his list of names.

"I'll be taking Manders with me and I want to see Ron Perry and Jerry Seymour – the two new families in the village proper, but first, I must get up to the Kellys. I have to see Hannah, but especially I need to see Dan, and the other Land Army girl up there … what's her name … Started with 'S'…Oh, yes, Sally Flinders!"

He looked up. "Oh, the youngsters are here now with the two extra cars. Off you go Potts – take one of the cars – and when you finish, come back to our headquarters at the pub."

Peters restrained Pierce. "Wait a minute, Sergeant, I want to speak with you." Potts climbed out of Peters' car as Constable Manders, his good looking face shining as usual with subdued excitement, took his place. Constable Potts was soon on his way along Tully Road.

"Pierce," instructed Peters, "when you join your driver, inform Constable Watkins on the whole situation – what Tim Johnson has said and, after that, I want you to show him the murder scene. These are two good men; they need every chance we can give them to learn. OK?"

"Sir." Pierce climbed out of the car and joined Constable Watkins who was waiting patiently at the wheel of the second car.

Peters sat in the car for a few minutes recounting to his own young constable what had occurred, with the information they had already acquired. He and Constable Manders had worked closely for a couple of years now and Peters had come to be aware of the solid worth of this young man.

When he had finished speaking, the inspector nodded, Manders dutifully started the car and was about to pull out into the street, when they heard a man calling, loudly and desperately, for them to stop.

TWENTY-FIVE

"Inspector, Inspector, wait a minute," the young voice shouted. Manders cut the engine and wound down the window. Peters looked enquiringly at the man, wondering who on earth this one was.

"I'm Ron Perry, Inspector, we're new to the village," the stranger announced breathlessly, "we bought the Nicholls' cottage."

"Indeed?" Peters responded, "I'm happy to meet you Mr Perry. Was there anything you particularly wanted? I'm in rather a hurry, but I did intend to call in to see you later this afternoon, but if it is anything important …" the Inspector left the sentence up in the air.

"Well, it's pretty important to me, sir," answered Perry. "You see, it's about the murder … you see … I knew the girl … I …" and, to the policemen's embarrassment, the young man broke down and started to cry.

Peters leapt from the car, opened its back door, and within a few seconds, had bungled the distraught man in the back seat out of sight of anyone in the street. Manders sat, staring straight ahead, utterly silent, his notebook on his lap.

Peters waited until the man gained some control of himself; while he waited, he looked closely at this newcomer to the village. His name had been on the list of suspects given him by Tim at the pub. Ron Perry was tall, good looking in a youthful way – could be much older than he appears, Peters thought – his hair was dark, almost black in colour, cut short and very neat, his mouth wide and his eyes startlingly blue. Black Irish, Peters decided, somewhere in his ancestry.

Perry sat up, wiping his eyes. "I'm sorry, Inspector; made a complete fool of myself, and out in the middle of the main street, as well. Hope to God poor Cassy – that's the wife – doesn't hear of it.

"The truth is, Inspector, I don't know how I could have been such a bloody fool, as to fall into her open-all-night trap – that is, Jean Harris, I mean, not Cassy – she's the best wife in the world! I know I'm not making much sense ..." he broke off. Manders in the front seat wrote unobtrusively in his notebook.

"Just take it slowly, Mr Perry," Peters calmly advised the man; realising that this man was genuinely upset; or, it certainly *seemed* as if he were anyhow. "Quietly and calmly tell me about it. I already know that you were intimate with the dead girl."

"Oh my God! That's already known?" the young man put his head in his hands. "What am I to do? This'll kill Cassy ... we've got four young kids ..." Peters decided on another method; no more sympathy. He spoke sharply, each word incisive:

"Mr Perry, I don't have the time to act as your nursemaid. You're a grown man, so act like one. Let me make it quicker for you. We know you knew Jean Harris; we know you were having an affair with her; we know you saw her last night in the pub; that she spoke to you and, I'm guessing here, you arranged to meet her outside the building, is that right? Yes or No?"

"Mainly, yes," answered the young man miserably. "Except that it was Jean who made the appointment, for me to meet her outside. I had made the decision to break it all off; I love my wife and kids and I realised I had been a complete idiot falling for this ghastly girl.

"I was aware that I could lose everything that was most precious to me, so I merely was courteous to her in the pub and she became furious. She then issued her ultimatum to meet her outside, or else."

"I see," Peters said, "she was blackmailing you? Threatened to tell your wife?" Peters then noticed the very expensive suit Perry was wearing. "Or, perhaps threatened to tell your boss …" Peters took a wild guess. "And, it's a pretty important boss at that, isn't it? Tell me his name."

"Sir Gerald Stone, sir, Head of the Ministry of Supply; I am his second in command." Perry answered vaguely, as if it were of little importance, "but no, she didn't threaten to tell *him*; she did threaten to tell my wife, but more terrifyingly than that: the head of the black market gang operating here."

"WHAT?" shouted Peters, rocked by this sudden revelation. "What black market gang? Are you a member? How do you know about it?" the Inspector hammered his questions, his voice savage.

"No, before God, I swear I'm not a member of it. But the dead girl was; she was in it up to her neck. When I had known her for a couple of weeks, she asked if I would be interested in earning some extra easy money. I immediately said I wouldn't.

"In my job, we're continually battling these gangs – so I guessed what she was going to say. When she told me about the gang, I was horrified to think that this peaceful village had a gang here. She told me it was flourishing; that there was really big money to be made. She said I was a fool not to 'give it a go' – her words – but, God forgive me, I said I didn't want to know about it – so I am guilty by omission, I know that."

Perry hung his head. "She also told me that our little escapades in the Oval at night, would be over if I didn't join the group. *At the time* I was totally besotted with her, and thought it was all probably a little light, 'under the counter' bargaining, that goes on everywhere; not big-time stuff – I truly never thought it was serious stuff."

"And last night you found out differently, didn't you?"

"You're dead right, I did," The man actually shuddered. "She was like a vixen last night. I told her I was not seeing her again, and she told me I *would* see her as often as she snapped her fingers; she also informed me that, as I now knew of the gang operating here, the Boss of the gang had informed her that anyone who informed on them, or attempted to leave them, was to be killed."

"Dear God," breathed Constable Manders, his pencil almost slipping from his fingers.

Peters stared at Perry, his face grim. "So, Mr Perry you couldn't get out of the mess you were in, so you killed the girl?"

"NO! God is my witness, I did not!" protested Perry, his face ashen. "I left her near the Feed and Grain store and actually ran home and told my wife I wouldn't be going to the pub at night any more and was sorry for leaving her on her own, with all the kids."

His eyes filled with tears again. "Cassandra was wonderful; being back home with her, I thought there is no greater fool than a man."

"Well, we've only your word for your innocence, and for what you said and what the dead girl said," Peters stated bluntly.

"And, I'm sorry, but it's not enough for me. You will now go with Constable Manders back into the pub, where we have our headquarters. You will make a complete statement of all your dealings with that young woman; he will type it up, you will read it and when I return, I'll read it and if correct, you'll sign it. You will wait in the constable's presence until I return."

Peters turned and addressed his colleague. "Manders, I'll go on to the farm. I'll return to see how you are getting on before I go to the other place I mentioned." Peters nodded with contempt to Perry.

"Get out of the car now; go with this constable. Consider yourself, for the time being, technically under arrest, until I read your statement. I'll then make a decision as to whether I shall take you back to the station, or let you go home. Out!"

Peters raised his eyebrows at Manders, who nodded and left the car. Peters slid over to the driving seat, noticing that Pierce and Watkins were still at the water-trough.

He started the car and drove quickly the short distance, stopping his colleagues just as they were about to leave. He tooted the horn loudly and the two policemen came running over. Peters rapidly filled in his sergeant on what had just occurred.

Pierce shared Peters' surprise and alarm – this enquiry was turning out to be more complicated than they had expected it to be.

"You can see why I was so desperate to see you, Pierce," Peters explained. "With this new knowledge you have, see what you can find out from those Yanks up at the Hospital – they could well be involved – they have access to goods we can't get. All right?"

The two policemen nodded and Peters set out for his long delayed visit to the dairy farm.

TWENTY-SIX

'Have you settled in now, Mrs Eckhard?" Annie asked, as she carefully studied what was still left on the shelves of the village general store.

The old couple who had owned the store most of Annie's life, had decided to retire and join their daughter in Wagga; they had sold the business to an Australian couple of German extraction, a Gertrude and Hans Eckhard.

Mrs Eckhard smiled at her customer. Annie had been one of the first to welcome the newcomers, with the unfortunate name, to their village.

"It was difficult, as you know, Mrs Watson. The work is nothing; we had a store in the Barossa Valley before, so that was no problem. But there have been other minor problems …"

"Such as your name?" Annie nodded her understanding. "I think you're simply heroic taking on a public job such as this, knowing what people will think and, worse still, *say*, about the dreaded Bosch."

"Even though my family has been in Australia since 1852," ruefully added the shopkeeper. "We expected trouble; there has been some, but not nearly as much as we expected … Some kids have been particularly unpleasant."

"Believe me, I can easily imagine that – I have no illusions about kids," Annie responded vaguely, her mind drifting to her visit to the

Valley when she was young. "The Barossa Valley is so beautiful I don't know how you could bear to leave it; my mother took me there when I was a young girl and I've never forgotten it."

"Yes, it is beautiful but Hans and I wanted a change; two of our boys are in the Army, one daughter is in the WAAF, the other is married and we only have the baby, Otto, now."

The woman laughed. "Please don't tell Otto I called him a baby! He's sixteen, strong as an ox and thinks he's a real man. He's still at school – can't wait to get into the Army; I'm hoping and praying that it'll all be over, when he's reached the enlisting age and that he'll go on to University; become a doctor, or a solicitor – but don't tell him that, either."

Gertrude Eckhard sighed. "Children can be a terrible handful can't they, Mrs Watson; they cause you endless worry and suffering; you're always on edge wondering what new problem's going to emerge.

"With the other kids in the forces, I thought it advisable to keep as busy as possible, in a totally new area, otherwise I'd drive myself crazy worrying about them."

"Believe me, I do understand that," Annie sat down on the stool by the counter. "And, every parent, if they are honest, will say exactly the same thing. And that goes for the English, the Australians and the German parents as well. And, dare I say it, for the Japanese parents also – though, I cannot be sure of that, as I do not know what the Japanese think about anything."

Annie shifted on her stool to get more comfortable. "You know what Mrs Eckhard? Although we've been through hell – brought about by the Germans since 1939 – I've never been able to feel any hatred for the *German* people.

"You see, when I was at school in Switzerland, we went for some wonderful trips. One was to Heidelberg; I loved it, as I did with Bavaria; I loved the people as well – the majority of them didn't choose that maniac as their leader.

"The ordinary German people are just people like us – I think of all the Mums and Dads who have lost their homes, their children, their loved ones and are in agony over their lives and their future – *if* the poor people have any future at all."

Annie rested her chin in her hand, her eyes tragic. "Mrs Eckhard, how do wars start? Here we have two *Christian* nations, killing each other; the soldiers on each side about the same age – most of them just boys, out of school – just like your Otto."

"You're absolutely right, Mrs Watson, and when I read earlier this year about the Bosch's *Second Offensive* beginning, this year, I couldn't believe it. 1944! It's insane! Europe is in ruins already! It will just mean more meaningless slaughter! Oh, it is terrible, terrible and what will happen when it is all over? There'll be nothing of Europe – or of Britain – left."

"I hardly dare to think," Annie said sadly.

The shop keeper looked at her customer.

"You are a remarkable woman, Mrs Watson," commented Mrs Eckhard. "And, a truly compassionate one."

"Rubbish! Most of the villagers are used to me – I've been here forever – and so they regard me as being the substitute for the village idiot – we don't have a real one."

The shopkeeper laughed. "Now, what did you want today?"

"Want? Anything you've got. There's not much on the shelves. No eggs yet, I suppose?"

"I'm sorry, no."

"Any butter?"

"No."

"Well, you'd better give me some of that hateful margarine. And, I need flour."

"Flour I have; margarine is now being rationed, so you can only have half a pound."

"Any tins of anything at all?"

"Well, there's some dubious looking tins of sausages; I wouldn't recommend them myself. God alone knows what the sausages are made of. At least, here at Mr Tanby's, you know the sausages are mainly bread, but the bit of meat in them is real meat." Mrs Eckhard leant forward and whispered. "I heard on the grapevine that they are using horse meat in the meat pies now; apparently the donkey population is now virtually extinct.

"However," the woman went on, "I do have something I can sell you." She winked. "A bag of potatoes fell off a lorry and it was offered to me. It's a bit more expensive than the usual, but I can let you have five pounds if you want."

"Potatoes? I wonder where they came from. However, I don't really care; I desperately need potatoes, as mine have now finished and until our new lot is ready to dig, I've very little to give poor Sam for his evening meal. Yes, I'll take five pounds of the spuds and be very glad to do so.

"And, if you have any, I'll have a couple of tins of that dreadful Camp Pie; it's terrible, but if you fry it in batter it's eatable." As Annie finished her shopping and was leaving the store, she stopped and turned back to the owner.

"Mrs Eckhard, a sudden thought struck me. Your boy, Otto, would have few friends here in the village – friends his own age, I mean. When my boy, Billy, comes home in a couple of weeks on vacation, Otto might like to come to our house and meet him. Perhaps, you never know, Billy might be able to persuade Otto that university is a good idea. What are Otto's main interests?"

"I'm sorry to say, Mrs Watson, at the moment they seem to be body building work at the gym, and rifle shooting."

"Oh, dear! I'm afraid he'd think Latin and Greek pretty poor substitutes wouldn't he?" Annie started to laugh, Mrs Eckhard joining in.

"I think you're right about that," the shopkeeper agreed.

TWENTY-SEVEN

When Inspector Peters had greeted Hannah and the Land Army Girl – who, he happened to remember just in time, was called Sally – he asked Hannah if he could use her phone; he had to get the medical report from the police surgeon. Hannah moved away so Peters could speak in private.

"Constable Clarkson, is everything all right there? I'm aware you're on your own, but we're flat out here and up to our ears … What? Who? Oh him! Tell him to go home and wait until I contact him, I know his problem; it's not important … Anything else? No? Good. Now listen. Has the medical report, or the preliminary report, come through yet? It has? Right, read it to me, slowly and carefully, so I don't miss anything.

"I see … alive before she went into the water, so was definitely drowned …Oh, a slight blow to the head…I missed that. Yes, I suppose so; blood would have washed off in the water … right …It makes sense, though; I was wondering how the murderer managed to get the girl's clothes off…Yes, you're right; blow didn't kill but enabled the killer to undress her and put her in the water…Right… Probably came to in the cold water…. Contents of the lungs? Good God, how revolting! Anything else, drugs of any kind? No, only some alcohol …What about time of death, any indication? Oh, definitely before ten o'clock and the doctor thinks could be from half past eight onwards but can't be sure, said if he had to make a guess, he'd say about half past nine … Well, half past nine o'clock fits in well, Constable, that's when she was last seen alive by a witness …

"Oh well, that could be very helpful … Thanks Constable. If there is more to come from the doctors, ring the places on the list that you have – Pierce told me he gave you our agenda when he rang for the other young blokes to come out here. You'll find us at one of the places or, if all else fails, you can always leave a message at the pub with Major Tim Johnson … Thank you – be in touch."

Peters hurried back to the kitchen where he found Hannah and Sally waiting for him. Dan came in and the men shook hands.

"Mrs Kelly," Peters began, "God help us, you've got enough on your hands and now you've got this murder as well. You were on our list as the first person to see this morning, but it has been a hell of a day so far, and this is the very first opportunity I've had to get here. I apologize for the lateness of this visit."

"That's all right, Inspector, I understand. Let me make you a nice cup of tea."

"To be quite truthful I was hoping you'd say that," Peters replied smiling. He turned to the girl.

"It's Sally Flinders, isn't it?"

"Yes, sir."

"Sally, I'm sorry that you lost your friend …"

"Sir, could I get something clear right at the beginning. Jean was no friend of mine. We were forced into the situation of working together and that's all. I am not a prude, nor am I some kind of religious nut, but I don't hold with the sort of life Jean lived and, to be quite brutally frank, I didn't like her much at all."

Fearing she had spoken out of turn, Sally blushed. "I'm sorry, sir, to be speaking evil of the dead; my dislike of Jean could well have been just plain jealousy – she was popular with the blokes, I was not."

The tea had arrived, and as Peters drank it, he looked with approval at the plump girl, with the work-roughened hands. "I think, Sally, you are an honest and decent girl and I can see from your very hands, that you are not afraid of work, whereas studying the dead girl's hands this morning I don't think she ever did much work here that really mattered."

Hannah broke in. "You'd be dead right there, Inspector," she declared emphatically. "She was a disaster from the very beginning. Why such a girl would volunteer for farm work, is beyond me. What the hell did she imagine the life would be like?"

"I agree. Well, now I have to search her room. I'm sorry to have to tell you, Mrs Kelly that I have found out things this morning about your lodger.

"But first, tell me this, have you been approached to buy large quantities of goods, especially food, or things that are fearfully scarce or unobtainable – that is, things on the black market?"

Hannah looked genuinely puzzled. "Honestly, no, Inspector I haven't. But then, we're not really short of food here; we are allowed to keep enough milk for ourselves and we can make the occasional butter; we grow all our own vegetables and, working seven days a week, we certainly don't need to keep buying clothes.

"I'd like to be able to buy new stockings and some new under-wear, but that's about it." Hannah put her hand to her chin. "But, Inspector, why are you asking that question? Is there some connection between Jean's death and the black market?"

"I'm dreadfully afraid there is, Mrs Kelly. I only learned a short while ago that Jean was heavily involved in a black market gang operating here in the village."

The three listeners were astonished. Both Dan and Sally had their mouths open in surprise. Hannah was nodding her head.

"That actually explains an awful lot," she said. "I wondered where, and *how*, that girl managed to get all those pairs of stockings, and underwear – you wouldn't believe how much she has. God forgive me, I thought she was getting it as payment – you know what I mean." Hannah blushed an unlovely red, and averted her head.

"Yes, I do understand. Well, Mrs Kelly and Sally, I want you to come and help me with Jean's room – I need witnesses, my constable is tied up elsewhere. Dan, I need to speak to you before I leave. Go on about your work; I'll find you when I finish here."

Hannah led the inspector into the bedroom of the dead girl, Sally walking last. Peters asked the two women to wait while he examined the bed.

Stripping it quickly, he folded the covers neatly and then lifted up the mattress.

"Eureka!" he cried. "It never ceases to amaze me that human beings nearly always hide things in the same places." He put the small book he extracted from the wire base in his pocket. "Now let's move on to the drawers and cupboards. Mrs Kelly, you and Sally, carefully go through the underwear drawer; that will be where the money is – *if* there *is* any money."

The three searchers worked silently and efficiently, starting with the drawers and laying each article in neat rows on the mattress. They were soon interrupted by a shout from Mrs Kelly. "Dear God! Look at this! I don't think I've ever seen so much money. There's hundreds here, Inspector! Good God! ... No! ...I'm not going to touch it! You take over now, please Mr Peters." Hannah moved away from the drawers her hands held high.

Peters quickly scooped up the money, neatly folded in rubber bands. He quickly counted it and asked both Mrs Kelly and Sally to witness the amount. "I'll give you a receipt for that amount, Mrs Kelly, before I go. Technically, as it is in your house, the money at the moment belongs to *you*. But, as I suspect it is the proceeds of criminal activity, it becomes the property of the State."

"Just take it out of my house, Inspector, that's all I ask," Hannah pleaded. "We're hard-working, honest people here; we've never had any tainted money in this house, and we never will."

She shook her head in wonder. "I really can't take it in; all that money and here we are trying desperately to just keep our heads above water."

The bedroom yielded no more surprises so Peters was able to move on to other matters. He asked Mrs Kelly if the Colonel had contacted her about milkers and was assured that they were arriving that very afternoon.

He then excused himself and hurried out into the yard in search of Dan. He had to get an explanation of that fight with Bianca last night at the pub. Then he had to get back to the pub where he had left Manders stranded with that Perry chap.

TWENTY-EIGHT

Constable Potts left the police car at the top of Quarry Lane, and walked the short distance to Bert Liveridge's house. It was nearly half way down the row of houses.

To Potts' surprise he found Bert tinkering with a very old truck, which was definitely pre-war. The top half of the vehicle was made of wood and had a sign, badly painted out, which still proclaimed itself to be a Baker's van.

To Potts' knowledge, Bert did not hold a driver's licence, let alone own a vehicle of any kind. He stopped and stood silently by the side of Bert who had his head in the engine, whistling tunefully. When he became aware of the policeman's presence, Bert reacted roughly.

"What the hell do you mean, sneaking up on a decent working man?" he demanded. "Come to have a look at my new acquisition have you? If you're decent I'll give you a lift back to the lock-up, if you like."

"Do you think we would make it, Bert, in that ramshackle old has-been?" Potts asked calmly.

Bert was incensed. "Isn't that just like the bloomin' lot of you? Jealous, that's what you are, green with jealousy. Just because I've come into some money, and can splash it around a bit; take the old woman for a spin in the country for a bit of a change, you're not happy until you're casting disparagin' remarks … Now, if only Tanya were alive …"

"Come off it, Bert. It's me, you're talking to," Potts shifted impatiently, on his feet. "Let's go inside, unless you want the whole street to hear my questions. Come on, I don't have all day; as a matter of fact I have an awful lot to get through before dark."

"Why should I come inside with you? It's bad enough you standing here in the street – blackening my good name with your presence. You'd better have a good reason for bothering me. What is it?"

"It's murder, Bert ..."

"Bloody hell! What do your mean? Murder! Whose murder? What are you talking about?"

"I'll say this one more time, Bert. Let's go inside now; otherwise I'll run you in."

"You'll what? What the hell has any murder got to do with me? All right, all right! I'm coming in. Keep your shirt on. Bloody Gestapo!"

When the two men had entered the house, Bert made a point of taking the constable into the front room; in previous visits they had usually spoken in the kitchen.

Potts had to prevent himself from goggling in his surprise, at the change in the room, since he last saw it. Everything in the room was sparkling new: the vividly patterned three piece lounge suite, the new, equally gaudy, carpet square on the floor, even the pictures on the walls. Everything was obviously and strikingly new ... and to Potts' mind, horrible. Expensive, trashy junk he thought.

Mrs Liveridge was dusting and greeted the Constable cheerfully. She was proud to be showing Potts her new treasures. Lily loved her small cottage and was so proud and happy, her elderly lined face glowing with delight at their good fortune.

"You see, Mr Potts," she explained, "we never could afford any new things before; always had to do with hand-me-downs, but since Bert came into his little legacy, we have been spending as we've never done before in our whole lives." Her eyes widened, "Oh, it's been wonderful!"

"Oh, give over, Lily," interrupted Bert. "This is only old Potts here, you're talking to, not anyone important. I don't think we should have let him come in the best room; the place for police is the kitchen."

Lily's aged, weary face clouded; Potts thought she would burst into tears at any moment. He could have belted Bert easily for his treatment of his wife, who had worked, either washing or cleaning, to keep him in comfort for the majority of their life together.

"Mrs Liveridge, your room is beautiful," Potts declared, addressing himself solely to the woman. "You have made it something really special. I can understand how proud of it you must be and rightly so, in my opinion." Lily smiled in appreciation and gratitude.

"However, Mrs Liveridge, I must ask you to leave us alone for a moment. I just want to have a quick word with Bert here, then I'll take myself off. I'm in a bit of a rush today."

The woman nodded her understanding and hurried from the room, shutting the door behind her. Potts' manner changed. He pointed his finger at Bert. "Sit down," he ordered, "or, I'll run you in. I mean it, I'm not joking!" Bert opened his mouth, but shut it quickly and sat down as ordered.

"You asked, Mr Liveridge, what murder and what it had to do with you. I'll answer you. It was the murder – a frightful and filthy murder – of your girl friend, Jean Harris last night …"

"Jean's dead?" Bert gasped, his face turning white. "But, I saw …"

"Exactly! You were seen …"

"Seen, seen where? Now, none of that, or I'll sue you. Yes, I admit that we had a bit of the old slap and tickle, but that's all. All right, I *did* speak to her last night …"

"At what time?"

"How the hell do I know? I don't keep checking my fob watch whenever I speak to anyone."

"Well, it must have been before a quarter past eight o'clock because that's when she left the pub."

"I remember now, it was early in the night – about half past seven."

"That's strange, we have a witness who saw you about that time nowhere near the pub." Potts kept his face expressionless.

"Oh, yes, I just remembered I had to pop into the Feed and Grain store to get some orders for deliveries they wanted done this morning. I saw Eric Munroe, he'll back me up."

"I see," Potts wrote in his notebook. "So, with the new sudden memory that has miraculously returned, what time did you get to the pub, speak to Jean, and where did you go after she left the pub? We know you didn't go home."

Bert had started to sweat. "Look, Potts, we've had our differences in the past, but you know me; you know I wouldn't kill anyone." Potts interrupted with a slight cough and raised eyebrows.

"I do remember a little matter of another murder victim, a Miss Tanya Illich, not so long ago …"

Bert quickly tried his best to cooperate by rushing into speech – anything to get away from the subject of Tanya Illich.

"Potts, listen to me. Jean came to me as soon as I got to the pub; we had a few words, she left early for some reason or other; she was not in a good mood and I did not see her again. I stayed in the pub until about half past eight o'clock.

"When I left the pub I talked outside with some of the men – Jerry Seymour was one of them I remember, then I came home. I did not see Jean again, after she left the pub and that's the solemn truth." Potts thought it was time to mention his philandering partner.

"And I am bitterly disappointed to discover not only you, Bert, but old Alf Cookson was also having a bit of a flutter with the flirtatious Jean. She seemed to be attracted to older gentlemen." Bert blushed scarlet.

"No man is ever too old to admire a pair of shapely legs and a pretty face. But, don't ask me about old Alf; whatever he did is his responsibility. I'm not his keeper."

"Well, I won't then. Let me ask you another question altogether, Bert. I want you to give me the name of your solicitor; then I'll discover the name of your benefactor who so kindly left you a bundle. I'll need his name for the inspector to check …"

There was a startled cry from Bert; to the Constable's eyes he looked truly ill. Rising to his feet, Potts said, "I'll get your wife to give you a drink of water, Bert, you look as if you need it. I'll be seeing you again shortly as soon as I've made my report to the inspector – he'll be *very* interested in you."

Potts quietly went to the kitchen, told Lily her husband was unwell, and would like a glass of water, assured her he would let himself out and made his way next door, to Bert's neighbour, Alf Cookson.

TWENTY-NINE

Sergeant Pierce decided he'd try to get the Americans at the Wembley Park Hospital over first – before he tackled the Darcys and the Moores in Quarry Lane. He was uncertain how long this would take and was also nervously aware of the difficulty he faced in dealing, not only with military personnel, but also foreign nationals.

In fact his fears were unfounded. Colonel Carter sent for the four men as soon as Pierce gave him their nick-names. The only condition he made to interrogation, by Pierce, was that he be present as a silent observer. Pierce thought this was very considerate and fair. Watkins came into the office with the Sergeant and sat unobtrusively in a corner with his notebook on his knee.

The four soldiers came in, one with callipers on one leg; one with a huge scar across his forehead – he had obviously suffered a horrendous head wound. The Colonel introduced the Americans to Pierce. It turned out that Spike was actually Ray Smart, Mitch was Michael Delaney, Andy was Andrew Holstead and Baz was Basil Robson.

The Colonel reminded Pierce that these four men were the ones he was sending to Mrs Kelly to help with the milking. Sergeant Pierce thanked the Colonel and the four men for volunteering to help that good woman.

"I'll not keep you long, gentlemen," Pierce began, "but your names have been given to us in connection with the poor girl who was murdered last night." The men looked embarrassed, quickly looking at each other and then at their superior officer.

"Could you just tell me, as briefly as you can, about the girl, Jean," Pierce put down his notebook and looked squarely at the four men. "Look, we are all men here; this is not an enquiry into your morals; we are only interested in anything you can tell us that can lead to the identity of the murderer.

"Let me make it easier for you. We know the kind of girl Jean Harris was, so nothing you can say will shock us. But let's get some details out of the way first: what time did you get to the pub last night?"

"Seven o'clock, sir," the man called Spike answered. "We were driven there by Captain Black – one of the doctors here."

"How did you get home?"

"The same doctor came for us at exactly eight o'clock," Sergeant Pierce looked at Watkins and breathed a sigh of relief. He, too, had rung the station and found out the time of death from Constable Clarkson.

"Did you return at all to the pub after returning to the Hospital?"

"No sir, we only had passes for the one outing," explained Mike Delaney, "but that didn't matter as we were all tired and, after a few drinks – Spike doesn't drink; he has lemonade – we were all ready for bed. We had to report to our Group Leader, Sergeant Lance Williams, before we went to bed."

Sergeant Pierce looked at the Colonel. "I think we can forget these men in any connection with the death of that young woman; she was killed between half past nine and ten o'clock." The Colonel nodded, pleased: one less worry he'd have to deal with. Pierce went on.

"Just one other thing I have to ask and then I'll leave you in peace. Have you heard of a black market gang operating here in the village?"

To Pierce's dismay, he saw a quick shuffling of feet and three pairs of eyes looked towards the fourth man, Andrew Holstead. The Colonel noticed it simultaneously and looked steadily at Pierce. He spoke courteously to the policeman.

"Sergeant … Constable … if you are agreeable, I think we can let Delaney, Smart, and Robson go, to start getting ready for their stint at Mrs Kelly's farm. Corporal Holstead, would you remain for a moment longer? Thank you."

The Colonel stood up; the three men saluted and left the room, leaving a white-faced young soldier staring at his feet. Sitting down again, the Colonel spoke grimly to the solider.

"Now, no shuffling about; get to your feet; stand up straight! Both Sergeant Pierce and I both want the truth and, by God, we're sure going to get it. Now tell us all you know of this despicable crime, which is what it is. If you are involved in this you have disgraced your regiment, your friends and your great nation … I'm waiting, solider … I'd advise you to speak quickly; you need to convince me of your part in all this, for you'll be facing a court marshal."

The young solider began hurriedly to speak, desperately trying to minimise his part in the whole affair. Watkins took notes at great speed, anxious not to miss one word of the soldier's testimony.

The Colonel and Pierce listened intently and when the solider had finished speaking, the Colonel reached for the phone and asked for the Military Police to come to his office.

Sergeant Pierce knew that his work at the Wembley Hospital was now over – the Military Police would now take over the case of Corporal Holstead. Pierce was both relieved and a little disappointed, at the same time.

As the two policemen walked back to their car, Pierce remarked philosophically, "Well, that's four of them we don't have to worry about anyhow."

"Makes it a bit easier, sir," Watkins agreed. "Now for the Darcy family?"

"That's right. Wouldn't it be nice if Alan Darcy suddenly confessed to the crime and it was all over, and done with?"

"Be a bit tame, sir," protested the young Constable.

"At my age, after all these years in the Force, son, I'm all for tame-ness," laughed Pierce.

THIRTY

Alexander Seymour had a happy little sleep up in the warmth of the bags of feed. When he awoke he quickly looked at his wrist watch – a birthday present from last year – and was relieved to see that the school bus had not yet returned to Bexford North. Alex stretched luxuriantly and considered his next move.

In his schoolbag he had pens and a bottle of ink, but he needed writing paper and envelopes; he knew where he could get them easily – from where he was lying, he could see them on the counter of the Munroe store. He slipped down between the bales and bags, and when the store was empty, hurried to the counter and removed what he needed; he then decided on another little experiment he wished to undertake.

As both men seemed busy carrying large bales outside, Alex took a small bottle he found among the animal medicines display section, emptied out the contents of the bottle, and quickly filled it with some of that very interesting anti-freeze liquid.

When he had heard old Charlie talking to Mrs Watson about how deadly the stuff was, Alex had an idea. Having sealed the bottle with its lid, he hastily returned to his position and, with great care, placed the poison bottle in his school bag – his mind dwelling pleasantly on the surprises in store for some irritating people.

While he was waiting for the time to pass until the bus returned, he composed his little epistles with eager anticipation. For the first time in his life, he was glad that he was good at school work; he could both read and write well; he also knew that his handwriting was highly above the standard of the other children; it was praised regularly by his teachers.

When he was satisfied with his composition, he started on his letters and wrote quickly and efficiently. After finishing the letters he wrote the name of the person carefully on the envelope, then added the words, 'For urgent attention' at the top left hand corner.

When he finished he had eight letters ready; he had decided to leave the Yanks out of it – he only had their nicknames – and that was no use – but it didn't matter, eight letters would be enough; his mind drifted to that smashing racing-bike he'd seen in the catalogue. Then he forced himself to plan his next move.

Alexander knew he would have to put these letters in the letter boxes himself, so he had to cover a fair bit of ground which he could only do on his bicycle. When he returned home this afternoon, weary after his fictitiously difficult day at school, he would convince his mother he was mentally exhausted; he needed a good run on his bike to clear his head, so he could do his homework.

She would believe that; she would believe *anything*, he thought contemptuously. Then he'd shoot off and get the job done. He would place a biscuit tin with a lid under the water-trough later in the evening.

The message he wrote on each letter was simple: 'I saw you with Jean Harris last night. Put one pound note in the tin under the water-trough outside the Feed and Grain store tonight, otherwise I shall tell your wife and the police that I saw you.'

It was only on three letters that Alexander left out the word 'wife.'

THIRTY-ONE

Constable Potts knocked at the door of the Cookson cottage. It was opened by Mrs Cookson who looked greatly relieved to see the policeman.

"Thank God, it's you, Constable Potts," she exclaimed agitatedly. "I simply don't know what to do and you are the one who can advise me. Come in, come in!"

She ushered Potts into their front room, where the Constable immediately noticed a very vivid and brand new, carpet square on the floor. He commented on this at once. Ada Cookson looked vaguely at the carpet and said something about liking a bit of colour; it brightened up the old furniture.

She was clearly distracted, Potts waited, knowing that she would tell him everything if he were patient.

"I'm sorry to have to tell you, Mr Potts, but Alf is not at all well at the moment. I don't know what has happened to him; but I think it's serious. I have him in bed and the doctor has promised to come, when he can spare a minute."

The old woman frowned perplexedly. "I simply can't understand it. He was as bright as a button early this morning, until he went out to the front garden and found a bundle of clothes – a woman's clothes."

Potts sat up straight; his mind racing. They would have to be from the dead body; nobody would throw clothes away today –

with rationing they're unprocurable!

"Tell me, Mrs Cookson, where are the clothes now? I'd like to see them."

"Well, that's the problem. When Alf picked up the clothes and brought them inside, I saw him stagger as if he was going to have a stroke. I asked him what they meant and he couldn't answer me; just kept looking into space and saying: '*No. No. No!*'"

The woman began to cry. "Mr Potts, what does it mean? What do the clothes mean? Why should Alf go all peculiar when he saw the clothes?"

"He's still in bed, Mrs Cookson?"

"He is; he hasn't said one word to me since he brought in those wretched clothes. Who could have put them there? It must have been overnight; why would they throw away clothes? What with the war and everything, no one throws clothes away today."

"Mrs Cookson, please get me the clothes; put them in an old pillow slip or something like that – a brown-paper shopping bag would do. I must take them; I'm sorry, but they are very, very important. Would you do that now; then I'll go and ring again for the doctor; I'll urge him to hurry to see Alf."

The elderly woman nodded and hurried from the room to return a few minutes later with a large brown-paper shopping bag bulging with clothes. Potts thanked her and kept the bag in his hand, holding it by the string handles. He then spoke in his official voice.

"Mrs Cookson, I know Alf is ill but I must speak to him; it's urgent." He stood up.

Ada was worried, her face puckered with concern. "He indicated he would see no one, Mr Potts, but I'm sure he didn't mean you – we've known you forever, we have … yes, come with me, I'll take you to him. You might surprise him – brighten him up a bit."

Potts doubted there'd be any 'cheering up'. He thought the 'surprise part' was sure to happen when Alf saw the clothes! He followed the woman into the main bedroom.

The old man in the bed looked expectantly for his wife when the door opened. However, when he saw Potts holding the bag, with clothes clearly showing from its top, Alf Cookson uttered a strangled cry of horror and gasping frightfully, fell back on his pillows.

Ada Cookson screamed, "Alf!" and kept on screaming his name. Potts, keeping the bag with him, assured the woman that he would go for help and rushed out of the house. He intended to head for the public telephone box at the top of the Lane, but saw Dr Edward Kemp's car entering the street at that very moment.

When the doctor stopped his car, Potts quickly told him what had happened, and Kemp hurried into the house while the Constable ran up the Lane, threw the bag of clothes into the police car parked there, then went to the Public Telephone box.

Constable Potts, having seen so many people die in his long career, rang for the minister, Mr Herbert Norman – Alf Cookson being one of his parishioners.

THIRTY-TWO

Inspector Peters found Dan in the barn lifting huge bales of hay and once again Peters was astonished at the strength of this young man. Dan stopped work when he saw his visitor and invited him to sit on one of the clean bales. Peters surveyed the young man carefully.

Dan was looking older than his twenty-two years and no wonder, Peters thought; his work load was extremely heavy. His black hair was thick and heavy. He was in need of a haircut, but that took time; he had no time to waste on vanity; Bianca apparently, trimmed it when he could stand it no longer. Dan's keen alert eyes were clear and unclouded and his mobile face had settled into a mature form; he was no longer the diffident boy Peters had encountered in that first meeting, years ago.

Dan was now most definitely a man: a man who was to be reckoned with. He was a strong man, strong physically and strong morally as well – which made all the more puzzling the hint from Tim Johnson that there had been something going on between Dan and the dead girl. Bob Peters went to work gently in a roundabout manner

"Dan, do you remember the first time we met in the de Lacey affair?" The young man laughed at the question.

"Do I ever? I thought at the end of it, my mother would've had your guts for garters!" Both men laughed. Peters sighed.

"Such a lot has happened since then Dan," He leant forward a little. "Tell me, is there any word from your brother Sean? Do you know where he is?" Dan's face clouded over.

"No, we don't. Every single day, Mum is waiting in the front yard, when Mr Norman is due with the mail – he's still our postman – but everyday he shakes his head and tells her the same thing: there's nothing." Dan's voice quavered a little. "It'll kill the old lady, you know, sir: poor bloody Patrick in a stinking prisoner of war camp with those filthy Japanese – whether he's alive or not, God alone knows? And, Sean, just *somewhere!*

"It must be the Pacific area I think; that's where the majority of Australian servicemen are now." Dan's face twisted in anguish. "It's the *not-knowing* that's the killer. In a way, knowing that Patrick's a prisoner is better, than not knowing where the other twin is. Poor bloody kid, if he's alive, he's most probably longing for a word from us, just as we are from him."

For a moment, Dan knuckled his eyes like a small boy, then shook himself, took out a cigarette and offered the inspector one. Peters shook his head.

"I think you're right about that, Dan; about the *not-knowing*. I certainly do know if it were my boy I'd be out of my mind – after all this time." Peters thought of an angle to get to the subject of the quarrel.

"Dan, your religion, and your mother's fervent faith, must be a help in the situation you're in, isn't it?"

"You're right. You know, Inspector, that's what brought Bianca and me together and I thank God for that. After we got the telegram about Patrick, Bianca comes to join Mum and me each night to pray for both the twins. She has never missed a single night; it can't be long as we both have so little time and she works so hard, the poor girl, but even if we are going to the pub for a drink, with perhaps a game of darts, she still comes here first and prays with the old lady and me before we set off."

Dan looked at the Inspector. "Sir, I've been so lucky with Bianca;

she's everything a man could ever want in a wife and our lives are so similar. She's there with only her mother and two sisters to do all the work in the nursery, while the stupid Government has her father and brothers interned, rotting in goal, sitting on their arses, just because they're Italian!

"Yes, I've been so lucky and, yet, do you know what sir, we had a stupid, stupid, stupid fight last night."

"Oh? No, surely not. What about?" Peters enquired innocently, his face bland.

"You wouldn't believe it; it was so crazy. Jean Harris and I have never got on since she first came here with Sally. Jean was so damned lazy, but she had a tongue on her – Bianca's is pretty hot as well,"

Dan smiled briefly. "Well, Bianca and I were having a drink when I asked her to forego the waiting, until her dad got out of goal at the end of the war and we'd just duck off and get married now – I was tired of waiting."

Dan pulled a face. "Bianca was furious; she said some cruel words, I added some, and just then Jean came over and asked me to be her partner in a game of darts. I stupidly said: 'Well, here's one girl that wants me, anyhow' and I went off with Jean to play the stupid game. Bianca said what she thought of that and I pretended to take no notice and began playing."

His face darkened. "When I looked over to where Bianca was sitting, I discovered she'd gone. I left Jean immediately; she became livid with anger and I went in search of Bianca, but she had gone off home."

"Did you stay at the pub when you discovered Bianca missing?"

"No. As you might recall, I'm not a good drinker; can't hold it somehow. So, feeling wretched, I left the pub to walk home thinking I'd been a bloody fool. To make matters worse, that ghastly Jean – God rest her soul, and all that – followed me out of the pub and continued calling to me until I was out of earshot."

"Where was Jean the last time you saw her, Dan?"

"Just near where she was killed – in front of the Feed and Grain store."

"I see," murmured Peters, "and you came straight home?"

"Yes."

"Tell me Dan," Peters asked quietly, "have you seen Bianca this morning?"

Dan smiled broadly. "Indeed, I have. She came here early this morning; we had just finished breakfast and I saw her coming across the fields. When she saw me she came running to my arms – all the silly quarrel was over. We were actually standing with our arms around each other, when Mum bellowed out that Jean had been found and that she was dead."

The inspector got up, thanked the young man for his time, asked him to say goodbye to his mother for him, and hurried off.

Dan seems in the clear, he thought; we'll just have to wait and see. But get a move on, he ordered himself. Constable Manders was patiently waiting for him at the pub; I shouldn't have left him playing nursemaid to Perry – he's too valuable.

I still have to get to that Seymour bloke; the others will be back at the pub at five o'clock. He was determined he would only spend a couple of minutes at the pub with Perry, then send him home; he wasn't likely to bolt – he could be 'left until called for'; from his performance this morning he didn't pose much of a threat.

THIRTY-THREE

Constable Potts was shaken by the apoplexy he had witnessed of his old friend, Alf, and after that experience, decided to try to get on with the job – there was nothing he could do for poor Alf and his wife.

He decided, as he was in the Lane, to walk back down and see that new Moore family. He knew it was on the sergeant's list, but the poor chap had so many to see, it might help if he gathered some information for him first. It's worth a try anyhow, the elderly policeman reasoned.

Reaching the end of the Lane, Potts paused at the gate to the small garden. Even though this family had not been there long – as far as Potts knew – they had certainly tried to get the old garden into shape. This boded well.

Potts firmly believed that a family who worked hard to make their house and grounds neat and attractive, were rarely the ones who caused the police problems – the theory didn't always work, Potts knew, but he liked to think it was the case.

He went up the two steps to the front door, which he noticed had received a nice new coat of paint, and the front windows were shining in their cleanliness. Potts was not surprised then to see, when the door opened, a very neat, tidy woman about thirty-three with brown hair, a welcoming smile who was attractive in a homely fashion.

She was wearing a floral apron over her house dress, but when she saw it was a policeman, she hurriedly removed the apron and smiled at her visitor.

Potts introduced himself and added: "You'll probably see me around a fair bit, Mrs Moore, I'm often in this area; been here all my life as a policeman. Is your good man at home?"

"No, Constable Potts, Toby is at work – at the munitions factory at The Junction; he'll be back about half past five, unless he has to work back. Can I help with anything, Constable? But what am I thinking of? Come in come in; I'm delighted to meet you; I've actually heard of you from Mrs Annie Watson whom I met at Mass at the Wembley Hospital chapel last Sunday."

"Oh, you know Mrs Watson, do you? Well, there you have the leader of this little village. A great lady, Mrs Watson – I've known her, and her late parents, all my life. They used to live in the Big House, you know." Potts was well launched on his favourite subject.

"Big House, Constable? What is that?"

"Don't you know? Well, the big Convalescent Hospital near the pub is called the 'Big House'; that's the ancestral home of Annie Watson, who was Ann Sheridan, the daughter of Lady Mary and Sir Joseph Sheridan – a very great family."

Mrs Moore was overcome. She leant forward breathlessly. "Well, I never! And there that great lady was, so friendly and welcoming; I never guessed she was from the gentry. Do you know, she was dressed so plainly, just like I am and I've seen her working in the orchard, as well as her garden, with a mattock and a shovel."

Potts laughed. "Annie Watson is as poor as a Church mouse; her father lost all his fortune, died, while his lovely and beautiful wife, the Lady Mary, frantically tried to salvage something from the wreck and built that little house where the Watsons live now."

Molly Moore clapped her hands in excitement. "Oh, it's just like the Pictures, isn't it? I should have known she was something special; her voice is beautiful and her speech is so refined. Are there any children?"

"Yes, indeed, there is a very beautiful daughter, Penelope, who married the local solicitor, Mr George McKenzie's son, George, who's a barrister; they live at Bexford, near the station. There's also a very clever son, Billy, who has a very serious heart problem, but has studied so hard he won a scholarship to the University of Sydney, where he's a great scholar."

Potts had no idea whether Billy actually *was* a great scholar or not, but he reasoned he had to be; he had won a scholarship to university and he was *still* there!

To Potts, a university was an exotic and inhibiting place; to actually get in there indicated that you had to be different from the usual run of human beings.

"But," Potts continued. "That's me just rattling on about your neighbours. Tell me have you settled in? Is your husband happy here? I think you have children for I noticed some bikes down the side of the house."

"Come into the kitchen, Constable, if you don't mind, and I'll pop the kettle on and we can have a cup of tea as we talk." She led Potts into a spotless kitchen, with sparkling linoleum, and urged her visitor to sit down and be comfortable.

"To answer your questions, yes we've settled in very well. Toby doesn't like the place as much as I do, but I think he'll come round in time. We have four children, all of them now at school – they'll be home soon – and we have nice neighbours … well … some of them are." Potts raised his eyebrows. The woman nodded and continued.

"In this little street – this Lane really – some of the people are very good and friendly people. I don't care for Mr Liveridge, but Lily, his wife, is a kind, hard working woman, so is Mrs Cookson. Her husband, Alf, is a very fine old man; he goes to Mr Norman's Church each Sunday. Do you know, Mr Potts, that kind minister came to welcome us, when we moved in, even though we're Catholics?"

"He's a good man, Mr Norman; that is exactly what he would do."

"I've met some of the ladies in the large houses in the village proper, also Mrs Kelly at Mass, of course, but I can only say I really feel at ease with Mrs Watson. At the top of this street, I'm afraid that I do not like the Darcy family,"

Mrs Moore hesitated. 'I know of nothing wrong about them, but I have heard the children swearing – really bad words – and I don't like that, Mr Potts. I'm trying to prevent my children from being too involved with the Darcy children, if I can possibly help it," Molly's face clouded. 'It's not easy, is it Mr Potts, to bring up children; to keep them safe, is it?"

"You're absolutely dead right there, Mrs Moore. Not easy to keep grown men from going astray either ..."

"Oh, I'm so relieved to hear you say that. You see, Mr Potts, I'm worried about Toby, my husband. I know it's normal for a man to go for a drink at the pub, after he's been working all day, but Toby is going most nights now, and I'm not always sure that it's the pub he's going to – it's not only children who can get in with bad companions."

Aware that she was possibly giving the wrong impression, Molly hastened to add. "Don't get me wrong, Mr Potts, Toby is a wonderful husband and a good father to the kids; I suppose I expect too much of men that's all."

"Well, we're a strange mixture I'll say that about us," Potts commented with a smile. "Tell me, was Toby upset by the murder of that poor girl, Jean last night – him being at the pub and all?"

"What a dreadful thing to happen in this lovely village! Yes, Toby was very upset; apparently someone had introduced him to the girl – but, what was she doing in the pub, I'd like to know; this war has had a very unsavoury effect on some women, hasn't it? I was relieved when Toby assured me he didn't know the girl, other than to just say hello to." Potts kept his face impassive, smiling benignly

The elderly constable stood up. "Mrs Moore you have been very courteous to me and I wish you and your family well. Your kind of family is the kind we want here. I'll have to be getting off, or I'll be in the bad books with my sergeant and my inspector.

"I hope you get to meet them, they're fine men – the best superior officers I've ever worked with." Potts extended his large hand and shook Molly's work-roughened hand heartily.

As he walked away a sudden thought struck him and he quickly retraced his steps and knocked once more on Mrs Moore's door. She was naturally surprised to see the policeman return, but he quickly told her about her neighbour, Mrs Cookson, and the shock she had just experienced, and asked if … perhaps … Mrs Moore might be able to help?

Potts was pleased that his estimate of the woman's character was correct: immediately the apron came off, she gave instructions to her eldest daughter, now just home from school, took four scones from a plate on the table, wrapped them in a tea-towel to keep them warm and hurried off to help her neighbour.

As he left the house for the second time, Potts thought: yes, a good woman, a good wife and mother. What the hell is Toby doing playing around with tarts like that Jean? Truly, men could be such idiots.

THIRTY-FOUR

Constable Manders sat still in the small parlour of the pub. His 'prisoner' Ron Perry was smoking incessantly; Manders had been forced to open the window – he was beginning to cough. He had refused the offer of refreshment from both Tim Johnson and his wife, but had permitted them to bring a glass of water, to Perry.

From time to time, Ron Perry tried to talk to the Constable, but Manders informed him, coldly, that every word he uttered would be written down, so it would be, in his best interests, to say nothing at all. The very stillness of Manders was intimidating to Perry; he had never seen anyone sit so perfectly still, yet so obviously alert.

In Perry's mind he was seeing all kinds of terrible images of impending punishment revolving in the stillness of the Constable's mind; in fact, he couldn't have been more wrong. Manders was slowly and carefully rethinking the entire picture he had seen the night before, forcing himself to remember every detail of what the main characters had *said*. He did this often; he found it aided his memory tremendously; if he wanted to get anywhere in the police force he knew his memory had to be kept as sharp as was possible. This was one way of doing it.

However, Manders *was* relieved when finally Peters hurried in the door. He stood to attention and handed to his Superior officer the typescript of Perry's statement. Peters read it quickly, told the suspect to read it and, if correct, to sign it. This being done, Peters then held the door open and told Perry to go. Peters kept his face expressionless and his voice cold. Perry attempted to speak; Peters silenced him instantly, closing the door on him. He then turned to Manders.

"Sorry, son, it must have been hell waiting all that time with that bloke. Couldn't help it; one disaster after another, but I sure needed you up at Kellys." He then proceeded to tell Manders of what he had found and took the huge amount of money out of his pockets – to the young Constable's stunned amazement.

"Now, my boy," Peters said, "as you've been locked up here for so long, duck out, use the Gents if you need; we have to leave immediately. I've still got to see the Seymours and I was hoping to see Mrs Perry without her husband, if that's at all possible – may not be, we'll see. Anyhow, let's see if we can get the Seymours done. Right?"

"Right, sir. Be with you in a jiffy," Manders dashed off to the Gents.

THIRTY-FIVE

Telephone call from Annie Watson to her daughter, Penelope McKenzie.

"It's only your old Grannie-Annie, darling … No, I'm fine, I was wondering how my granddaughter is … Blooming? Well of course she would be, wouldn't she? She's going to be the exact duplicate of me … Really! Penny, I had to hold the receiver away from my ear; I am appalled to hear such language! … Now, to be serious, dear, are you still involved in 'Food for Britain parcels'? … Yes, I thought you were …

"Well, just between the two of us, we have a couple of wealthy new families in the village, the Seymours and the Perrys … No, … Public Service; very high-up positions – lots of lovely cash … Well, my dearest, I thought next time you're out here, you might like me to introduce you to them; you can twist their arms, as it were – in a ladylike manner of course … I think your best bet would be Mrs Seymour – her name is Elise – I know she desperately wants to belong, so I'm sure she'd be interested in being asked. Mrs Perry is wealthy enough … but she has four very young kids so might not be able, simply through lack of time … Anyhow, dear, just a thought; I know you're always looking for new members.

"Now about our murder … yes, it made all the papers … sensational stuff, the papers loved it – naked young woman, filthy horse-trough, bad reputation, lots of men suspects … blackmail's been suggested … Yes, very exciting, it's a wonder that I'm not interested in it, isn't it? … Don't say 'yeah' in that disbelieving voice dear, it's so very American; though I have to admit, with so many Americans here in the village, from the Hospital, I've got into the bad habit of saying 'guys' when I mean men. I've discovered that they, the Americans, actually use it for both men and women – a sort of common gender … weird, but then Bernard Shaw had a lot to say about American English, didn't he? …

"What? I haven't even mentioned it have I? That's how hard I am trying not to even think about it. I thought of making George a bullet proof vest just in case; don't suppose he'd wear it though … Seriously dear, is it getting him down, the constant surveillance by the police? No? …Thank God for that.

"Any more phone threats? No? I'm being serious, please tell me, Penny, it's better knowing than imagining things … I see, so the threats are continuing … Darling, would it be safer if you and George moved back here, until the wretched trial was over? … No, I suppose George wouldn't agree – men are so difficult. I know Harriet and her George would love to have you both – with my granddaughter as well, of course.

"All right, I'm going … praying constantly for you darling … and for George. Billy told me to tell you, if I was speaking to you, that he's going well, coping with the studies so far and has remained fairly well; only missed a couple of days, so keep your fingers crossed … Must go, darling, I have to work out a plan for the meeting at the pub with the ladies … yes, the Occupational Therapy group. Bye, dear."

THIRTY-SIX

Elise Seymour was disturbed to find the police on her doorstep. She was hesitant about inviting them in. She quickly looked up and down the street, then over at Annie Watson's house, to see if anyone was watching the police car at her door.

"Mrs Seymour," Peters introduced himself, "I am Inspector Peters and this is Constable Manders. We want to speak to your husband for a moment or two, if he is available. You remember, I'm sure, he and I met earlier when he was doing a sterling job guarding the body of that poor young girl who was murdered." Peters had moved forward slightly. "May we come in, or would you prefer we had our meeting out here in the open? I always think it better not to give unnecessary reasons for neighbours to gossip, don't you?" Mrs Seymour moved away and led them silently into the front room. When she spoke it was in a carefully controlled, refined voice.

"I'm sure, Inspector, you gave me quite a shock when I opened the door. We are certainly not used to having the police at our door. My husband is, as I'm sure you know, a very important man in a Government Department."

"Yes, he made quite a point of telling me so, Mrs Seymour. May we sit down? Thank you. Won't you sit down yourself?"

"No, thank you, the children will be home from school any moment now, so I'll just see if my husband can be disturbed; he's engaged on some very difficult Government work in the study.

Excuse me." Elise hurried from the room and the two men looked at each other, and smiled.

Peters looked carefully around the room. It bore no trace of the humble, simple room it once had been, when it was owned by Miss Amelia Tatley. Now, it was the epitome of expensive furniture – and little taste in both furniture and furnishings.

However, it spelled out clearly that this was a wealthy household – where expense was no object. There were pastoral scenes in gold frames on the walls, a beautiful antique book shelf with a set of books on it that looked as if they were never to be opened, one shelf of exquisite ceramics and a beautiful, and obviously expensive, arrangement of artificial flowers that was almost successful in convincing you they were real, not just lifeless imitations.

Soon there was noise in the hall; Peters and Manders hastily stood up as Jerry Seymour entered the room.

"Sorry to keep you waiting, Inspector, just finishing some wretched forms – they have become the story of my existence, ever since the war began." Gerald sat down, stretched his legs out comfortably and looked expectantly at the policemen.

"Shoot, Inspector. Have you found the murderer yet? Only joking; tell you what, it gave me a hell of a turn seeing her in that filthy trough."

"Yet, you knew her well, didn't you Mr Seymour," Peters said, sitting down again.

"When you say 'well' I suppose just as much as anyone who goes to the pub would."

"Oh, I beg your pardon," Peters apologized. "I have heard it said that you knew her intimately – as in the Biblical sense of 'knowing' – not just as a passing stranger."

Seymour's face darkened. "Who's been talking? I'll belt their heads in. What are they saying about me? You can't trust anyone these days. Go on, tell me, what are they saying?" Peters put on his conciliatory look.

"Well, I'm sorry to have to say it, but it is said, that you were having an affair with the girl, Jean Harris."

"What!" Seymour jumped up and shut the door of the room quickly. "Keep you voice down," He sat down again. "What if I did have a spot of the old, 'how's your father', with Jean – she was over twenty-one and ..."

"And, you are a married man," concluded Peters quietly. "Listen to me, Mr Seymour, we are not here to hold a morals investigation – in spite of all your protestations this morning about your moral integrity, referring to the minister, Mr Norman – which incidentally, I didn't believe for a minute. All I am interested in, is clearing up the matter of the girl's murder."

Jerry Seymour's mood had altered. Gone was the assurance and swagger he had shown on entering the room. He looked nervously at the inspector.

"What do you want to know?"

"Did you kill the girl?"

"Oh course I didn't! What a question!" Seymour laughed nervously.

"Well, what time did you leave the pub last night? You were seen talking to the girl and, if you like, flirting with her at the pub, so when did you leave?"

"Leave?" Seymour was pondering. "It's bloody hard to remember isn't it? I mean you don't spend all your time looking at your watch when you're relaxing. I think it would have been about half past eight, or a quarter to nine o'clock when I left. I spoke to some chaps outside ..."

"Their names?"

"Names? Well, there was Bert Liveridge, Alf too; I think, then there was one of the Yanks also, Holstead, I think the name is; his first name is Andy."

"What time did you actually get home?"

"About ten o'clock I think; can't be sure. I'd had a skinful – more than usual, and was a bit groggy. Tell the truth, that's why I'm home today. I rang through to my boss, said I was feeling seedy and asked if I could I finish the forms here at home. He's a good old codger, and he said it was all right."

"Ten o'clock," Peters repeated his face expressionless. "Make sure you note that Manders."

"Sir."

"Now just one more thing Mr Seymour," Peters pretended to read from his notes. "There is a rumour going about that there is a well organized black market gang operating in this area, have you heard of it?"

Seymour sat up straight. His voice was suddenly outraged. "No! The black market? Good gracious, that's a dreadful thing. No, I haven't heard of it. How would I? Everyone knows I'm connected with the Government – I'd be the last to know."

Peters raised his eyebrows in surprise.

"Oh, I thought you would be the first to hear of it, Mr Seymour, through your relationship with Jean Harris. She was in the thick of it. Apparently Jean Harris was the treasurer of the gang."

Gerald Seymour looked ill. He had turned quite white. He stood up.

"I must ask you to excuse me, gentlemen. This has been a dreadful shock to me. I had no idea that Jean was into anything like that. If my name is linked to anything like this I don't know what old FC would say. I'd be ruined."

"By FC, I suppose you mean Sir Frederick Courtney? Yes, I thought so. He's a personal friend of my Acting Commissioner." He stood up, Manders did likewise. "That's all for now, Mr Seymour. But, because of your relationship to the dead girl – with her connections to the gang – we'll most probably have to call and see you again; there's bound to be more questions to ask." He moved to the door, "Please don't bother, the Constable and I will see ourselves out."

The policemen left Jerry Seymour standing in his gilded surroundings, angry and fearful. He muttered to himself: Bloody hell! I've got to get those blokes to shut their mouths, or we're in for it.

THIRTY-SEVEN

The Seymour house was next to the Tanby butcher shop. Outside the shop Mr Tanby, the butcher, was speaking to a young woman with four young children. Peters noticed the young woman and made a shrewd guess.

"Manders, I bet that's the Perry woman. Look, we might be lucky for a change. Hurry up, let's 'accidentally on purpose' meet her." He walked quickly to the butcher.

"Good afternoon, Mr Tanby," he called, moving forward and holding his hand out.

"Why, it's Inspector Peters," Tanby declared smiling. "Inspector, I'd like you to meet one of our new families. This is Mrs Perry. She and her husband and all these little treasures have come to live in old Major Nicholls' house. Mrs Perry, this is our very famous – and a good friend of the village – Inspector Peters, and, if I remember rightly, Constable Manders."

Mrs Perry, a pretty, young woman smiled shyly and shook hands with both men.

"I am happy to meet you gentlemen. That is what I like about this village. Everyone knows everyone and is so friendly. I can only hope we stay here forever; it's a beautiful place to bring up the children. The people are so welcoming.

"Do you know what, Inspector Peters? Mrs McKenzie – she lives next door to us – has invited me to join their Occupational

Therapy group for the Convalescent Hospital; I'll be going to their meeting tomorrow morning – Ron, my husband, will be minding the children."

"That's splendid," Peters replied. "The McKenzies are wonderful people, and, of course you would have met our famous Annie Watson, I'm sure." Cassandra Perry smiled.

"Indeed I have; she came to see me; the first one of all. She'll be at the meeting tomorrow."

"Really? That's excellent. Now, I wonder if you and I could have a little chat for a moment, Mrs Perry, about this dreadful matter that occurred here this morning. We could just walk along here. Don't worry about the three children who can walk. Constable Manders here is an absolute wonder with children, aren't you Constable?" Manders looked panic stricken, but nodded bravely, "so he'll take the kids and walk behind us. All right? Let me carry those groceries – you've got your hands full."

Peters and Mrs Perry, carrying her youngest child, led the strange procession back to her house with Manders, at his wits end, trying to control three young adventurous infants lagging behind. He tentatively picked up one child, leading the other two holding hands, while a large wet patch began slowly spreading down the front of his uniform. It was fortunate that Manders had a highly developed sense of humour.

He found himself laughing silently at the ridiculous picture he was making of himself and only hoped that Constable Watkins, who would by now be up at the Darcy house, didn't come back in time to see him.

THIRTY-EIGHT

Sergeant Pierce, a family man himself, was appalled to see the condition of the Darcy house as he and Constable Watkins were led inside by a slattern of a girl, dirty and vulgar looking, who was unsuccessfully trying to conceal the cigarette she was smoking when she had opened the door.

The building smelled of dirty clothes, cabbage, cigarettes and alcohol. The girl informed the policemen she was Buffy, was fourteen year of age and her mother was not yet home from work.

"And, you … er … Buffy … not at school today?" enquired Pierce, clearing a place on a chair to sit down. The girl yawned. "Nope, finished with all that; fourteen years and nine months, last month." She yawned again to show her boredom, aware that now she was of legal age to leave school, she was safe from truant officers.

"I see," remarked Pierce seriously, "and are you thinking of studying for a special job; something you'd really like to do?"

The girl stared at the policeman as though he were demented. "More study? Who me? What on earth for? I'm going into the munitions; that's were the money is, believe me, not in some stuffy job, and …" the girl winked intimately at Watkins, "that's where the fellows are too." This was followed by a knowing laugh. Watkins was scandalised and had great difficulty in keeping his face expressionless. He was dismayed to see a child – for that's all this girl was – so clearly marked out for a life on the streets.

"And where does your mother work ... er ... Buffy?" asked Pierce.

"Up at the big Hospital; works in the kitchen, she does," again the girl laughed that dreadful knowing laugh, "brings home some super food, she does. Lot of Yanks up there; Mum like Yanks."

"And your father?"

"He's the one who works in the munitions factory. On day-shift now; should be home soon. Hope the old woman will be back before he comes home, or there'll be another row. What did you want to talk to them about?"

"Nothing much, Buffy. Only to see if your mother could tell me whether your dad was home last night." Buffy laughed, a loud raucous sound this time.

"You must be joking. How would she know? She wasn't home last night; out with her bloke I imagine ... and him? He would be seeing his little flash piece, that Jean girl with the long red nails."

"Are you telling me you know this, or only making it up," Pierce demanded, sternly.

"Course I'm telling you. I was left to look after the bloody kids wasn't I?"

"How many other children are there," Pierce's voice had softened in pity for this poor, wretched, abandoned, girl-woman.

"There's two others: Ollie, he's twelve and Harry, he's four."

"And you look after the children yourself, Buffy? I think that's a pretty wonderful thing you're doing."

"Well, it might sound that to you; I hate it. I hate my parents and my whole family, too. As soon as I can, I'm getting out. The only one I really love in this hovel, is Mingy. I'm taking her with me when I go."

"Mingy? I don't remember that name among the children."

Buffy laughed again. "Silly! Mingy's my cat." She reached under the sofa and dragged out a ragged looking, half-starved cat and hugged it close to her chest.

Pierce coughed while Watkins stared at the opposite wall. The sergeant quickly changed the subject.

"About Mr Alan Darcy, your father. Will he be home soon? I'd like to see him if possible."

"Shouldn't be too long, then he'll be off to the boozer, or to some of his pals; doesn't spend too much time here at home. Come to think of it, neither does Mum."

"Well, Buffy, we'll be getting along. It's been nice meeting you. Would you ask your mother and father to call us at the pub, when they get home? You must be anxious to get back to your work in the kitchen. You do most of the work in the house, don't you?"

Buffy looked indifferent. "Mostly. Used to it I suppose. I try to make sure I've got something cooked before the old folks get home – they like their food. The other kids make do with what they can, though I try to see they get something good to eat at night. They usually don't eat breakfast; Ollie makes do at school by pinching other kids' lunches – he's a tough bastard."

She drew on her cigarette, not caring now, whether they saw it or not, "Seems to work out all right." There was the sound of the front door opening and Mrs Darcy came in, yelling as she did so. "Where the hell are you, you lazy bitch? If I find you haven't cleaned the kitchen, I'll …" she had reached the front room and stood still.

Mrs Darcy was a thin, attractive woman wearing brilliant lipstick, high heels and a short skirt, with her dyed blonde hair in a turban. Her clothes were smart and she wore real silk stockings Pierce noted. After her initial shock, the woman went on: "And, who the hell are you, and what are you doing here, alone, with my daughter? I'll report you to the police, I will."

Buffy laughed. "Come off it Mum. They *are* the police, so pipe down will you?"

Mrs Darcy stopped her tirade, suddenly trying to save the situation. "Well, I wasn't to know that was I? Buffy … I mean … Rosemary … have you made the gentlemen a cup of tea?" Her eyes were signalling frantically to her daughter.

Pierce informed the woman they were about to leave. They only wanted to know if she were home last night and could verify that her husband was there also.

Mrs Darcy immediately said she was home all last evening; she didn't go out at night, leaving the little ones alone; what kind of mother did they think she was? Her husband, Alan, was with her; they played dominoes after they had listened to the evening news. Watkins wrote every word down as quickly as he could, only his eyebrows indicating his astonishment at the lies.

Buffy began to laugh helplessly. "Too late, Mummy dear! I've already told the police that you were out with your boyfriend, while my dear, dear, father was with his bit of skirt, that Jean girl – the one that got bumped off last night." A new thought struck her and she laughed, even more loudly. "What do you reckon? Do you think Dad bumped her off? That'd be a lark; that would."

Mrs Darcy moved forward, her face furious. She raised her hand to slap that impertinent face, only to have her wrist grabbed by the Sergeant. "I don't think so, Mrs Darcy. At least one person in this house tells the truth, that's clear. You will be hearing from us within the very near future, Madam. We'll let ourselves out."

They left the house which was suddenly strangely silent behind them and drove back towards the pub. Pierce decided he would have to leave the Moore family, until the next day. Peters would be waiting for them.

THIRTY-NINE

By five o'clock all the policemen were sitting gratefully drinking black tea in the small parlour of the pub. The publican had the tea ready a few minutes after they had all arrived. Peters gave the men a little while to collect their notes on their day's activities, and then he began to speak.

"I'll start with my own report to keep you up to date. Potts, I'm sorry but something happened after you had left, so I didn't have a chance to tell you. So here goes." Peters told of Perry's surprising confession of his affair, openly admitting he saw Jean after she had left the pub last night; that he had an argument with her; he then had astonished them by informing him there was a black market gang flourishing in Bexford North and that Jean was heavily involved.

At this point there was a loud exclamation from Constable Potts. "Bloody Bert Liveridge's new front room! I knew there must be something wrong going on! Sorry, sir to interrupt; I'll come to it later. You're in for a surprise, believe me."

Peters continued, recounting his visit to Kellys. He took the actual money from his pockets and laid it on the table. The other policemen gasped in astonishment. Peters mentioned the discovery of a book hidden under the mattress, informing the men he intended to study it that night. He also mentioned how helpful the girl, Sally Flinders, had been, as well as Mrs Kelly.

He revealed the details of the argument between Dan and Bianca, which also put Perry and Dan outside with Jean at the incriminating time. Peters had then to recount his meeting with Seymour; his conviction that he was heavily involved in the gang, so must be included in the group with no alibi for the time of the murder. Peters concluded with his walk home with Mrs Perry, who confirmed her husband's account of what he said, when he returned home last night and she seemed utterly naïve in regard to his involvement with the girl, Jean Harris.

The atmosphere had become heavy, as the full weight of evidence began to accumulate, so Peters lightened the account, with his story of the heroic Constable Manders, his long period as a jailer and finally, his adventures as an infants' child minder. "And," he concluded, "he's actually wearing on his uniform, the scars of battle." which made all the men laugh, including Manders.

Pierce's report was much shorter. He spoke of the long wait they had at the Wembley Hospital until they could see Colonel Carter; the interview with the four American young soldiers then added, "You'll be delighted to know, Inspector, that we can eliminate four men from our group of suspects for the murder, as they have an iron clad alibi for the time of the death."

"Thank God for that," responded Peters. "What about the black market?"

"That's another matter, entirely, sir. It seems certain that Corporal Andy Holstead is definitely involved. However, as soon as that emerged, the Colonel pulled the shutters down, rang for the Military Police and we were politely shown off the premises,"

"I see," murmured Peters, "disappointing, but in a way it could turn out better for us; from twelve suspects, we now have only eight and the army police methods of interrogation would not be so hampered as ours are. If there is something serious to find out, they'll soon get it out of the silly lad. I am confident that Colonel

Carter – who's a sensible man – will let me know, one way or the other, if it seriously involves people from the village." He looked at Pierce. "Anything else?"

"Yes, sir, the Darcy family," Pierce turned to his constable. "Watkins would you like to do that one?" The young man nodded and faced Peters.

"Sir, the family is a disgrace. I believe it's a case for intervention by the Child Protection authorities. I firmly believe that the girl left running the house *and* looking after two other kids – one, only a baby in nappies – could be categorized as being 'exposed to moral danger'."

Peters looked at Pierce. "Do you agree, Pierce? What exactly is the situation up there?"

Sergeant Pierce, who was as horrified as Watkins had been, described the scene in the Darcy's house in detail; the girl Rosemary, called Buffy, the other two children, the filth, the smell, the mother with her boyfriend; the father with his carrying on with Jean – all well known to the fourteen year old girl. The child had placed yet another man at the right place and time for Jean Harris' murder.

Pierce made a suggestion at the end of his report. 'I think, sir, we should contact the woman police officer at The Junction and ask if she could call at the house, and investigate the situation. I think she should be accompanied by a man – that couple could easily be violent."

"Will do, Pierce," Peters promised. He looked at his old friend, Constable Potts. "Potts, I suspect you are sitting on a bombshell. I'm waiting to hear all about it, so stand back fellows, Constable Potts has the floor."

Potts laughed. "Inspector, I do have some pretty important stuff to say for once. I was just lucky I think. I went first of all to our old friend, Bert Liveridge," there was a collective groan at the mention of the name, "and would you believe it, little Bertie has had a legacy, or so he assures me.

"He now has a truck – a *truck* no less, therefore *petrol* – and you have to see his front room to believe it: everything in it brand new; all in vivid colours, even a brand new carpet on the floor. Horrible actually, but terribly expensive. Poor Lily thinks she has died and gone to Heaven. Poor woman has never had anything in her life; now she's got all this new, ghastly stuff – thinks it wonderful. Poor, unfortunate woman, I told her I thought it was beautiful – God forgive me.

"Bert was obnoxiously rude as usual and I felt like thumping him, but when I got him alone I questioned him about Jean. I think we can forget his involvement with the murder; he seemed genuinely astonished and frightened.

"I reminded him of his previous involvement with the death of Tanya Illich; he didn't like that. Then I asked him to give me the name of his solicitor, so we could learn who his benefactor was. He turned white and I had to get Lily to get him a glass of water. I said we'd be seeing him later."

"So, he's definitely involved, heavily so, by the sound of it," Peters commented. "The truck is interesting; who would suspect an old codger like him of transporting stolen goods. I bet the truck is a wreck, is it?"

"Spot on, sir," confirmed Potts. "But I haven't finished yet. I went from there to Alf Cookson." Potts' honest face looked worried and upset. "Ada, Alf's wife, told me Alf was ill in bed – she had sent for the doctor – and Alf had only become ill when he found …" Potts reached under his chair, and held up a shopping bag full of clothes, "these clothes planted near his letter box overnight." There were gasps of surprise again. Peters started to laugh.

"I knew you had something under your chair. You were so careful to keep your legs in front of it so I couldn't see, you old devil. They *have* to be the dead girl's clothes, don't they?"

"I'm sure they are, sir. They're women's clothes, everything she wore, including her shoes – nearly all brand new. Who'd throw out good clothes today? A deliberate plant on the poor old man, I think."

"You're absolutely right, but by whom? Ah well, we'll find out eventually. Go on Constable."

"Well, God forgive me, I didn't mean to frightened the poor old chap into a fit, but I insisted on seeing him and when poor Ada led me into the room; one look at me and Alf gave a dreadful cry and fainted dead away. Thank God, Dr Kemp came just then, and I hurried up the lane and phoned for Mr Norman. I think poor old Alf might have had a stroke."

Potts sighed, "But I think we can take it for granted that he *was* involved, not in the murder, but in the black market – perhaps just keeping quiet about it – for he, too, has a vividly coloured new carpet square in *his* front parlour as well – but that seems all he got out of it."

"Dear God, Potts, you have done better than any of us. Any other startling news?"

"Only good things, sir. I knew that the Moore family was on the sergeant's list, but I thought I'd visit them and do some of the ground work. They seem an exemplary family – the wife is anyway – house beautifully kept, kids clean, nicely spoken, very respectable woman, a *real* Church-goer, knows Mrs Watson and Mrs Kelly, tries to keep her kids away from those terrible Darcy children.

"However, Mrs Moore is definitely worried about her husband, Toby. I think it's fair to suggest that Moore's eye is definitely wandering, so we'll have to keep him in the picture – for Jean's murder – he was at the pub last night. It's such a wonderful, respectable family to see – especially these days – that I think Toby would do anything to avoid his name being connected with Jean. That's all, gentlemen."

"And there Constables, you have just been given a perfect report of a day's work by an experienced man who notices everything. Well done, Potts." Constable Potts actually flushed with surprise at the praise; he said again that he had been just lucky.

Peters wound up the meeting. He made it clear he wanted all the men back on duty in the morning. They were to arrive at the pub at nine o'clock; with luck they might be able to leave early in the afternoon. He informed them that he would have the policewoman there from The Junction – they would attend to the Darcy matter without delay. He stood up and the men made their way home having been granted permission to keep their cars; they would need them in the morning.

Tim Johnson came in as Peters was leaving the room. He informed him that Mrs Watson was on the phone and would like to speak to him. Peters hurried to the office and was surprised and delighted to hear Mrs Annie Watson invite him to have dinner that night with them. She said she had something she wanted to talk to him about.

Peters courteously accepted the invitation and, as he hung up the phone, thought ruefully: I know damn well what that's about. Ah well! There's nothing much more the police *can* do about it, more's the pity.

FORTY

Alexander had no difficulty in persuading his mother to let him go, as she phrased it, 'for a nice little bicycle ride'. The boy had the letters carefully in his top shirt pocket. He had decided he would pretend to be taking a rest as he leant against the letter boxes; it would be easy to slip the letters in without anyone being the wiser.

As his bedroom window opened onto the actual lane leading to the Oval, he would slip out though the window after the evening meal when it got dark and wait, hiding near the trough. He would then see if anyone had opened their letter that evening and arrived to do as he had ordered. This was quite probable, as many people did not look in their boxes until late in the afternoon when they arrived home from work.

He began with the Perry letter-box; that was a breeze; then rode very fast to the dairy at the Kelly's place. He then had the tricky Quarry Lane section to do. He decided to do the last house first, so rode quickly down the lane to the Moore house, slipped the letter into their box then, pushing the bike back up the footpath, panting as though exhausted, he slipped a letter into the boxes of Liveridge's and Cookson's.

Alex now only had the Darcy house to do. He thought this could be awkward; those blasted kids were always running around the place. Hurrying past their house, he saw that mongrel cat sitting on the top of the letter box as usual. Alex hated cats, and each time he and this particular cat had met, he had been scratched. He managed, however, to get the letter in the box before he was seen and before he was *scratched – your* days are numbered cat, he muttered.

A tough twelve year old boy, named Ollie, hailed him and Alex was forced to talk for a little while, but he pretended that he'd get a terrible flogging if he didn't get back home. Shooting off from there, he only had Eric Munro and his own father left to do. Before he entered his own front gate, he slipped the letter under the door of the Feed and Grain store, then finally, dealt with his own letter box. With his heart glowing with the satisfaction of a job well done, he wheeled his bike around the back of his house.

Feeling happy and excited, Alex realised he was hungry and was now ready for his evening meal.

FORTY-ONE

Both Hannah Kelly and Sally Flinders studied the three American soldiers who turned up to help with the milking. Dan hurried in and the men introduced themselves quickly to Dan and Hannah, who shook their hands vigorously.

Hannah made it clear, in a 'no-nonsense' voice, that Dan was in charge and would tell them what to do. Sally was introduced by Hannah, as an experienced and totally reliable milker; she would be able to help, if the men had any questions.

The soldiers were dressed in Army fatigues, so they didn't look as glamorous as they usually did in their well-fitting uniforms, but Sally, carefully looking at them, thought they were fine looking men, especially Spike, the one with the calliper on his leg.

She was particularly assiduous in taking him with her to the milking shed, personally showing him where to sit and suggesting ways in which it would be easier on his leg while milking. He clearly was overcome with such attention and blushed frequently.

Hannah watched the whole proceedings with amusement. She thought, without their uniforms, they looked just like any other ordinary self-conscious young men. They didn't appear overly intelligent, or educated – in fact, they looked exactly what they were – ordinary rural boys from a farming background. As she carefully kept an eye on the milking for the first hour, her worries regarding their competence subsided; they certainly were not unfamiliar with cows – and their ways.

With the three extra helpers, Hannah, for the first time in years, was actually free to just supervise, so when everything was going well, she went back to the house and began making another big batch of scones, as after the work, the men would be hungry. She regretted she had no jam left, but she had Golden Syrup and she knew men liked that on their scones.

She would insist they stayed for a cup of tea, before they walked home, back to the Hospital. She wished she had coffee to give them, for they were Americans, but she didn't even have that awful imitation stuff – hickory essence, or some-such-rot. It was so revolting that nearly everyone simply refused to drink it.

Sally was in her element. Without the very attractive Jean, she was chatting freely with the soldiers as they all worked, answered their queries, even before Dan could frame a reply. Dan smiled and with a shrewd perception of the situation, let Sally show the men the ropes.

Spike, whose real name was Ray Smart – as he confided to Sally – was particularly grateful to the girl; he thanked her with a shy smile, every time she helped him. Sally blossomed and actually revealed, for the first time since arriving at Kelly's farm, her true self. From time to time as the assorted group milked and called out to each other, Sally's eyes drifted to the Spike boy, wondering if he had a girl back home, or not.

Perhaps, he was as lonely as she was … Perhaps, as he would be here each day …Perhaps …who knows…

FORTY-TWO

"That truly was delicious, Mrs Watson," Inspector Peters declared, as he finished his meal at the Watson's house.

"Thank you, Mr Peters," Annie responded, "one day, when this ghastly war is over and there's real food on the shelves again, I promise you I'll cook you a meal you won't forget, for then I'll have something to cook *with*." Peters smiled, beginning to take his plates to the sink, only to be prevented by Annie.

"No, you don't; you've been working hard all day. Take yourself into the lounge and sit for a while with Sam. I'll be with you in a moment or two, with an apology for this awful, dreadful and almost undrinkable liquid, which they insist on calling coffee – I can't imagine what it's made of; perhaps it's just as well we *don't* know."

When Annie carried in the coffee later to her husband and the policeman, she broached the subject that was uppermost in her mind.

"You must know, Mr Peters, about the situation with my daughter and the security problem for her husband George McKenzie?"

"Oh course, I do, Mrs Watson. As it is in my area, I was consulted from the beginning of the problem. As soon as Mr McKenzie took on the Prosecution of that gangster at the trial, I knew there would be trouble. Why the newspapers have to publish the names of the legal teams, in trials like this, I cannot begin to comprehend. I can understand your worry and Mr Watson's, also the McKenzie's, but there nothing much more that the police *can* do."

"That's what I told the missus, Inspector," Sam said, "but, Annie was insistent that something more could be done."

"The truth is, Mrs Watson," Peters explained, "in these situations, you can take all the precautions you can think of and you can still be out-manoeuvred. The horrible reality of the matter is: if someone is determined to assassinate you, there is really little you can do to stop it. You can only do your best to cover every *obvious* probability."

"There's no way you can talk sense into the young couple, is there; tell them that you think they would be safer if they returned home?" Annie asked.

"*Would* they be safer here, than in Bexford? I think it would be easier to shoot someone here, than it would be in a heavily built-up area – perhaps not. However, I did suggest to the relevant authorities exactly that, but both Young George and Mrs George strongly rejected the idea – said they would not have people saying they were running away."

Annie sighed. "Oh, such stupid pride! As if that matters in such a situation. Why are young people so stupid? Ah well, we've done what we could. I couldn't leave it without asking your advice." She changed the subject. "Tell me, how's the murder going?"

Peters smiled, his voice amused. "I heard, on the grapevine, that you were not taking any more interest in murders and such sordid things, Mrs Watson."

"That's true – in a way. However, I'm insatiably curious and just wonder if you have covered all your bases. Have you seen everyone you think may be involved yet?"

"No, we haven't, not yet anyhow. It was a vile murder, a dreadful death, made worse, in my mind, that no one really liked the poor girl. I suppose that's true of many murder victims, but it makes me have sympathy for the victim for some reason."

"What about her parents? I thought they would have been on the scene, by now."

"I think they're all noise. They apparently blasted poor Mrs Kelly, on the phone, basically accusing Dan of the killing as I told you, but we haven't heard a peep out of them since."

Peters pulled one of his rueful faces. "I shouldn't be telling you this, but I will. I rang Newcastle Police and asked them about the parents of Jean; that I had expected they would have been down here like a shot when they heard their daughter had been killed. The police, however, knew the pair, it seems; they laughed. They actually *laughed*.

"They warned me that it would take the complete Japanese invasion to get Brian and Beryl Harris away from the race track tomorrow. They warned me that, once the Saturday races were over, I'd probably have to deal with them – they wished me luck."

He sighed. "Really, human beings are the strangest creatures. Children are so precious and yet they are often treated so badly. Even today, Sergeant Pierce found … oops! Sorry, that's classified." Peters looked guiltily at the Watsons. "Please Mr Watson, Mrs Watson, forget you heard me say that."

"I know whom you're talking about – it's the Darcys," cut in Annie. "We oldies have been talking about that family, wondering what on earth we could do to help. That very nice new lady, Mrs Molly Moore, alerted me to the situation, Inspector, so don't worry, you are not revealing anything we didn't know. If the police are doing something about it, they have my full support."

Soon after this conversation, Peters made his farewells, thanking his hosts, not forgetting to ask about his young friend, Billy – now at university – and then enjoyed the luxury of driving home in the police car.

His mind reverted to the book belonging to the dead girl which he must study before he went to bed. He sighed; this could be yet another late night.

FORTY-THREE

BW dialled a local Bexford number, using a public telephone box. "You know who this is? "

"Yes… Thank God you're rung! The situation's now arse-up; what are we to do?"

"Well, for the moment, I've had word to lie low now she's dead. You understand?"

"Blimey, don't I?"

"However, we're short of just on a thousand quid; we've got to recover that, the boss will go ravers."

"How? The police have been to her room; they will have it by now."

"Bugger! Are you sure of that?"

"Yes, their car was seen at Kellys; obviously searching the place."

"That's torn it. Let me think …"

"There's another problem …What about … you know…"

"What?"

"The goods. We can't let them be found now, can we?"

"Of course not, I'm trying to work out how we can shift them. Do you think Bert will still cooperate and do a quick run with the old truck? It'll have to be either tonight, or tomorrow night. We can't wait any longer."

"I don't know about Bert; he's got the shakes after the constable's visit."

"Well, he can shake as much as he wants, but he's got no option; tell him that, will you? And tell him he knows the penalty of squealing; he'll wonder what hit him."

"When you say move them, move them where?"

"I'll have to ring AF. He'll tell me where there's a safe place for the time being."

"Are they still in the empty annexe to Charlie's store?"

"Yes, not that the pompous Victorian relic, knows they are."

"Well, is it tonight, or do we leave it till tomorrow?"

"Let's make it tonight – anything could happen now; we dare not let the stuff be found. Bert will need a couple to help him shift the goods – there's a lot of stuff there. Get help – don't take no for an answer – and organize it yourself. I'll find out where the Boss wants it to go and you ring me in half an hour. Right?"

"Right! Before you go; one more thing. Now the tart's gone, do you think we should try using the other one – you know, the fat one – as we did Jean?"

"It's possible; you could see if you can chat her up when she comes to the pub. It's worth a try. Okay?"

"Right."

The line went dead.

FORTY-FOUR

The winter evenings brought the dark quickly and in the blackout – which had lasted for years now – Alexander had no difficulty at all in slipping out his bedroom window, crossing to the Feed and Grain store on the opposite side of the lane. There were some tall empty drums near the water-trough and with the blanket he had brought with him, Alex took shelter behind the drums, covering himself up, prepared for a long wait.

A half hour later, Alex was delighted to hear stealthy footsteps approaching the area. For the first time he felt a little apprehensive – it would be all right wouldn't it? Holding his breath, Alex heard the footsteps stop at the trough, then the tin being taken up and the snapping sound of it opening and closing; finally the footsteps receding. He jumped out of his hiding place and hurried to try to see who the person had been. In his frustration he quickly discovered, with the blackout, he couldn't see any person in the street. No matter … he'd see how much money they'd put in the tin.

Alex had a small pencil torch – he had swapped some unwanted comics that he had outgrown, for the torch – and quickly opened the lid of the tin. Peering inside, he wanted to yell aloud in his delight. There was a one pound note in the bottom of the tin. That was a small fortune to the boy; he realised, with trembling excitement, this was just the beginning. Tucking the note into his trouser pocket, he scurried back to his hiding place and covered himself again, with the blanket; his mind a whirl of happy anticipation of a big spending spree in the future. He started to doze and was soon sound asleep.

FORTY-FIVE

Mr George McKenzie stood waiting in his kitchen, his wife Penny with him. They had finished breakfast and were waiting, silently, in the early light of the morning. Normally the Court did not sit on Saturdays. The Judge, however, deemed this trial too important, also too dangerous, to follow the usual procedure for the weekend. The very large number of police, who were responsible for the security of the jury – as well as the witnesses for the Crown – were very anxious this trial be concluded as quickly as it could be, without compromising the demands of justice.

George, breaking the silence, took his wife's hand. "You'll be all right, Penny, won't you? Promise me ... No foolish worrying. They've given me every protection possible. I can't even go to the lavatory without someone with me. I can hardly wait until this blasted trial is over, then we can have our normal life back again."

"It can't be over too soon for me, dear," Penny sat down quickly on the kitchen chair; terribly afraid that she would have to rush off quickly – this morning sickness seemed to be going on forever. Penny was worried George would think there was something seriously wrong; that she was ill. She smiled up at her tall, worried husband.

"He's late, George, isn't he?"

'A bit, I expect. He's a good chap. I don't know how they put up with it: all this cloak and dagger, dodging about they do …" he was interrupted by a discreet knock on the door.

"All ready, sir?" a tall man in an old cream, well-worn and slightly soiled, overcoat, a battered hat and thick black-framed glasses came quietly into the room. "Sorry, I'm a bit late. The car's here."

"Not to worry," George replied. "Let's change and get going. This part always makes me nervous, for some reason or other." He laughed with nervous tension. The two men rapidly changed coats and hats, then the glasses and, within a couple of minutes, a very smart look-a-like Mr George McKenzie left by the front door, with his 'wife' standing waving him off as he left in the car, while a rather disreputable man, with black-framed glasses, wearing an old, cream overcoat, collar turned up, with an equally battered hat pulled down low on his head, left by the back door, walked around the block, joining the main crowd of people hurrying to the railway station. He was soon lost to sight in the crowd.

FORTY-SIX

Alexander rose early, after returning to his bed via the window well after midnight. He had been disappointed that only one more pound note had been found in the tin but he reasoned, in all probabilities, tonight would be the better night – the letters would have definitely been found and read by then..

Creeping out of the silent house, Alex rode his bike quickly, in the early light of a crisp winter morning, to Quarry Lane. He left his bike around the corner of the Darcy house, in Tully Road and walked to the letter box where he found the cat, again perched, waiting for the first rays of the winter sun.

She hissed as usual, when she saw her tormentor but the boy held out to her a small piece of meat. The cat stopped her menacing noises and became interested in the food.

Alex carefully put it on the ground at the foot of the post. The cat leapt down and found that there was a little liquid surrounding the meat which smelled even more appetising that the meat. She rapidly began to lap the fluid while Alex hurriedly returned to his bike, and rode home.

By the time he had reached his house the cat was in its death throes, its body twisting and writhing in its agony, screeching insanely, before it fell over. Alex had been reluctant to leave the Darcy house; he would have liked to see the cat die – that would've been fun, but, unfortunately, it was too risky.

However, he was sure the poison would have worked quickly, just as old Charlie Munroe had told the Watson woman it would.

FORTY-SEVEN

Annie Watson knocked loudly on Florence Armitage's door. It was answered by a pretty young girl who smiled when she saw who the early visitor was.

"Amy-Lucy, I know it's early, but has her Majesty arisen yet?" Amy giggled, and said she had.

"Well, Amy-Lucy, please tell her that her interfering friend, and *expert* medical adviser, has called, demanding an audience with her, will you?"

"Oh come in Annie," called a voice from the morning room, "and stop frightening the maids. You know perfectly well that it is Amy, not Lucy, so stop calling her Amy Lucy."

"No, I won't," Annie answered stoutly. "While the twins persist in looking so alike that no one can tell the difference, I shall continue to stay on the safe side and call them both, Amy-Lucy; it has a fifty-fifty chance of being right." Annie had reached her friend by the end of her sentence.

Florence Armitage was a heavily pregnant woman of remarkable beauty, who was nearly forty years of age. She was expecting her first child very soon. Annie had monitored Florence during her entire pregnancy, calling in nearly every day checking on her friend. Their close friendship had been forged, in tragic circumstances some years ago, when Annie had befriended the extremely wealthy, lonely woman, who became involved in a very unsavoury murder.

Annie had remained Florence and her soldier husband, Stephen's, greatest friend and confidante ever since. Florence had a highly developed sense of humour, and regarded her balloon shape with hilarious amusement. She had a flair for colour and clothes and looked wonderful even in the state she was in. She was cared for by two twin girls from the Orphanage run by Annie's Aunt, the Lady Benedicta Sheridan.

Annie sat opposite her friend. "No more jokes, Florrie, dear," she said quietly. "How is it going? Any pains yet? Has the baby shifted at all?"

"It's certainly shifted, Annie," Florence replied. "I'm sure it's a boy – the kicks it gives me are quite extraordinary! I think he's going to be a footballer," She smiled. "Just wait a few years, then he'll get a few kicks himself when I remind him of how he treated his poor old mother."

"So, it's still waiting?"

"Afraid so, Annie. Dr Kemp said everything is fine, but even he admitted that he'd be glad when it was over. Let me tell you a secret, come closer,' Annie leaned closer to her friend, 'Edward Kemp told me he's arranged with Dr Waters, down at the Convalescent Hospital, for me to go there, if everything happens in a hurry,"

"Oh, I'm so relieved to hear that. Sister Rumpit is still there and she was magnificent with Susan's first one. That's one worry out of the way. Do you know if they'll let Stephen have some leave when your time comes?"

"Stephen doesn't know yet, Annie. He's hoping they might. But I thank God every day for my two girls – they have been a godsend to me, not just with all the work of this huge house, but they're so funny and chirpy that they've made this period of waiting one of the most enjoyable times of my life."

"Well, I can't be just sitting here gossiping, Florrie, I've got a meeting with the ladies at the pub this morning. We're going to change some of our activities at the Hospital. Have you any ideas yourself?"

"Well, Harriet McKenzie told me about the meeting and I've been thinking of it. I have some ideas. They came after I met that new woman, Mrs Perry. She told me she had been in an Amateur Dramatic Society at Uni. She has actually played in a number of productions which were directed by her husband – that's how they met. Well, I did wonder if you could work towards producing a type of concert – not a full play, but something with songs, perhaps some barber-shop quartet stuff, skits – things like that."

"I like it. It's a novel and interesting idea. Nan Brady could easily handle the singing bit. Perhaps we could do something in a foreign language, perhaps French. I was thinking of German, but perhaps that's a bit off. Anyhow, you've given me a lot to think about." Annie leant forward and kissed her friend lightly on the cheek.

"Don't forget: have Amy-Lucy phone me instantly after they phone the doctor – if there's the slightest change in your condition. It will almost certainly be within the next day or so, dear." Annie stood up. She called out loudly to the maids: "Amy-Lucy, if you're sure you're finished drinking the cooking sherry, come and let me out." The maids came giggling, trying to remember their training, as they ushered 'Madam' out of the house.

As Annie walked down the steps, she prayed God to grant Florence a speedy and easy delivery. With Dr Kemp she, too, would be very, very, relieved when it was all over.

FORTY-EIGHT

Inspector Peters sat in the small parlour of the pub waiting for his men to get there. When they did arrive, complaining bitterly of the dreadfully cold morning, with its freezing wind, they huddled around the open fire which the publican, Tim Johnson, had again thoughtfully provided for them.

After greetings were exchanged, Peters made the men sit down and opened the book he had found in Jean Harris' bedroom the day before.

"Now, men, listen carefully to this. It's very important as it concerns the black market activities in this area. I think it reveals, not only the extent of the activity, but it seems to shed light, in a fairly obvious manner, on the identity of the murderer; but, it's possible, we could go wrong here." Peters turned to the page he wanted. "Now listen carefully," he ordered.

"You'll see, in a moment, how the girl organized her accounts. She seems to have been given two jobs: one of recruitment officer and the other of accountant – perhaps *treasurer*, is a better word.

"On the first page here is the list of 'Goods received' from someone called BW for a mysterious AF. I'll read you the description of the goods, as written here:

1 ton Bed-socks

10 doz. Slippery stuff

20 prs Legs eleven

30 doz Billiard balls

2,500 Contained cows

1,000 gal Mechanical starters,

4,000 Passes for different rides,"

"What the hell! Excuse me sir," Potts' eyes were goggling. "What on earth is she talking about?"

"Well, Constable," Peters smiled, "she's definitely not talking about bed-socks. As you all would have realised, the words are a code; they mean something else – something that is impossible to buy today with rationing. We'll get to that later.

"The next important page is the distribution account. Apparently, most of the goods went to the shops at The Junction. I think we could guess some of them. When we are certain, we'll raid them in a joint exercise with the chaps at The Junction.

"The shop initials are: BLW, CO, HH, TW, PSg. – they're the ones at The Junction, and there's an AE at Bexford itself.

"Now we come to the wages of those involved. Jean – on paper – anyway, meticulously accounts for every penny. She appears – at first sight – as being scared stiff of trying anything on the big boss, but I suspect that's all a smoke-screen. I think she was ripping them off. Here are the main figures and initials; you can study the rest at your leisure:

"Firstly there is an acknowledged receipt of £1,000 from this mysterious BW who's obviously acting for the big boss AF. Then come the initials of each person who shared in this large amount of money: how much money they received – or goods in kind – then the tally of how much is left over from the wages pay-out. Listen carefully:

BL £175

AC £20

AD £105

GS £467

JH £110,"

Peters looked up from the book. "Next to that last amount, which clearly refers to herself, the girl had written: 'Insist on more; I do all the work; deserve more; let GS know – he can contact BW,' Now, going on:

TM £105

AH 20prs. £20

OE –xxx

RP –xxxxx

Total for June/July paid out: £1002. Overpaid by £2 (to be reimbursed to JH in next payment Aug/Sept)"

Peters stopped again, and looked at his colleagues. "Nearly finished now; the last entry concerns the removal of the goods – from an unidentified location wherever they are stashed – to somewhere, unidentified, at The Junction."

"Blimey," ejaculated Sergeant Pierce, "there's been a roaring illegal trade going on here under our noses, obviously big by the amounts you have read out and we didn't have a clue about it. Doesn't make us look very good, does it?"

"No Pierce," Peters agreed, 'it does not. However, if it's any comfort, just about every police station in the city is experiencing the same situation today. But let's sort out the people involved. I'll read out the initials and you tell me who they are. Most are pretty easy.

"BL? Yes Potts?"

"It wouldn't be our old friend, wily Bert Liveridge, by any chance, would it sir?"

"Fancy that, Constable, you're dead right, I'll bet a quid." Peters smiled at his old friend.

"TM"

"Tony Moore," Potts said sorrowfully, thinking of his good wife.

"AC?"

"Alf Cookson, sir." Manders was the quickest off the mark, but all of the men knew that one.

"AD?"

"Alan Darcy." Watkins got in first, looking pleased; not forgetting what he had seen yesterday at Darcy's house.

"GS? Now, be careful, we're on to the big one here."

"Has to be Gerald Seymour, doesn't it, sir?" Pierce said.

"Well, it certainly has to be, as far as I can make out. That is, of course, if all the punters are from the village, but what a risk he was taking! Working for such an important Government Department and under such a stickler as his boss – a man of unimpeachable integrity. Let's go on.

"AH?" Potts was quick with this one. "That American soldier, I think the name was Andy Holstead."

"That's what I think, Constable." Peters looked at the second last letter on the list, his face perplexed.

"OE? Any taker?" There was silence in the room. The men racked their brains trying to think of anyone local who had those initials. Finally, Constable Potts said hesitatingly, "There's … the German boy, of course … but that's ridiculous."

Inspector Peters was puzzled. All the men looked at the elderly Constable with surprise. "German boy?" repeated Peters, "What German boy?"

Potts looked confused. "I didn't mean that he *was* German – but the name is German." No one looked any the wiser. It was Watkins who suddenly realised what Potts was saying.

"Sir, I think Constable Potts means the boy belonging to the family who bought the local shop. They have a German name; it's Eckhard. Is that it, Constable?"

"Yes, that's the one. I knew the new people had a German ancestry but they're been in Australia for generations. Most of their kids are in the Forces but they have one son at home; his name is Otto."

"OE! Potts you're a genius!" exclaimed Peters. Potts laughed.

"No, not a genius; just happened to meet Mrs Eckhard when I was in buying some pipe tobacco the other day. She told me about her children."

"How old is this son who's still at home, Potts, do you know?"

"He's sixteen, I think."

"Oh, just a school boy. Any reason, Potts, why we should follow him up?"

"Well, Otto is a male; he's sixteen and, from what I've heard, is a muscle bound young bloke, who excels in professional shooting matches; apparently he's a highly trained rifle shooter; he's also a boxer – he trains at a gym and he's had a few amateur junior fights."

"Good gracious," Peters frowned. "I was picturing a young, gawky boy with glasses and pimples. Let's leave him in then, chaps. You'll notice he does not have any money after his initials."

Peters looked squarely at his men. "I'm sure the RP is Ron Perry, but can anyone of you guess why there are only 'Xs' after his name and not money."

Manders flushed slightly but held the inspector's eye. "Could it be that both he and the unknown person, OE, did not receive any money at all, but received, could we say, 'goods in kind' that is, privileges, from that enterprising young woman." The young Constable then added: "and if young Otto is the OE we're looking for, then it would make even more sense."

"I'm certain that's the only conceivable answer. It's all I could make of the X's after the names, anyhow. I'm sorry, really, about Perry. I think he's a decent chap normally; I suppose the 'privileges' you speak of, Manders, were for keeping his mouth shut about what was happening, if he really knew much about it at all. I'd be inclined to think he didn't; he was simply besotted with that woman."

"And, for young Otto?" Pierce queried.

"Well, it easy to imagine what he had to gain from the association with Jean. However, I don't think he would be involved in the black market ring, as it would be too dangerous to include someone with such a hated name, as that poor young chap has."

"I agree totally with you, Inspector," Potts said. "That poor family have suffered so badly from insults, especially from kids, since they came here, with some very cold-shoulder treatment from the villagers as well. If the boy, or the family, were involved in the gang, most of the others would refuse to work with them – *because* they're German."

"So why would Jean bother with the young bloke," asked Pierce, then blushed furiously. "Forget I said that; I understand exactly how tempting she would be to a young virile male, at that age."

The inspector stood up and walked around the small room. "Well, what are your thoughts? Do we round up these characters in a group? Have we enough evidence to arrest them? What do we really have? I suppose it could be argued that all we have is the fanciful writing of a nymphomaniac – I can hear the defence counsel saying that ..."

Pierce interrupted the inspector.

"We have the money, sir. No Land Army Girl could have that enormous amount in her drawer, but ... Hey, just wait a minute ..." he paused, his eyes widening in surprise.

"I know where you're going, Sergeant and it's worrying me as well. Let's see if the youngsters see a problem here, I bet Potts does. Well, Watkins, Manders?"

The two young constables looked blank, for a moment, and then struggled to be the first to speak:

"Sir, why did ..." began Watkins, while Manders finished the question:

"... that girl have all that money in *her* drawer? I thought you read that it had all been paid out."

Potts clapped his hands. "Give the boys a cigar, sir, they've deserved it." They all laughed.

The elderly constable continued. "So Jean was on the fiddle, sir. She was either paying out less than ordered, or else was falsifying the results for the sale of the goods. It has to be one or the other; no one has that sort of money lying around in their drawers today."

"Exactly, Constable. I think that's the reason for her death – although I have to admit that Annie Watson does not think money comes into the picture. She said it was a passionate crime and involved betrayal. However, I think Jean had either been found out, or else, she got cocky and put into practice her demands for a bigger cut in the profits. If either of those two things happened, BW, whoever he is, would never stand for that and, remember, Ron Perry told us that if anyone got out of line, they were threatened with death by the big boss, whoever he is."

"Sir," Sergeant Pierce intervened. "I'm worried about the other persons with just initials. That is BW and AF; there's no one here in the village that I can think of with those initials. They must be outsiders."

"They puzzle me also, Pierce …" The inspector was interrupted by a loud knock on the door. Watkins quickly opened it and an agitated Mrs Kelly came charging in. The men stood up as Hannah marched to the inspector.

"Inspector Peters, will you be just looking at this now, will you? As if my poor lad hasn't suffered enough; to think that he's now accused of killing that lazy, good for nothing girl. 'Go to the police', they threatened. Well, I grabbed the letter from Dan and said I'd certainly go to the police all right. What have you to say about this?" Hannah thrust a letter in front of Peters' nose.

"Please sit down, Mrs Kelly," Peters gestured to the young ones to bring forward a chair. "I don't know what you're talking about …" Peters began to read the note.

"It's my boy, Dan … as if …"

"Ssh! Please Mrs Kelly, just let me read this note … Well, I never!" He looked up at the anguished woman. "Mrs Kelly, do you mind if I let the other men see this note? It's very important. It means we have a blackmailer involved as well as everything else." Taking her silence for consent, Peters quickly handed the note around.

"Mrs Kelly, is Dan upset about this?"

"Upset? No. Angry? Yes."

"And I can understand that! Mrs Kelly, by bringing this letter to us, you have actually foiled the blackmailer's little game; he can't hurt you, or Dan, anymore; he has no more threats to make." He stood up. "Mrs Kelly, please don't be upset. We'll get to the bottom of this I promise you. Go on to your meeting – Mrs Watson told me about it last night. Just try to forget this. However, that's easy to say I know. Thank you for bringing it to us. Watkins, the door. Oh! ... Wait a minute, Mrs Kelly, are you good at crosswords?"

"Crossword puzzles? Is the man mad? What time do I have for crosswords?"

"Well, I have a problem which only a woman such as yourself can answer, but she must be good at crosswords."

"Then it is Annie Watson you need. She's the one with the brains," Hannah smiled. "I'll tell her you need her for a few minutes." Hannah nodded to the policemen and hurried to her meeting.

FORTY-NINE

Annie Watson was happily introducing the new people to the group of villagers assembled for the meeting. Annie was in her element and, being as unexpected as usual, had introduced the two women to the same people several times. It became such a muddle, that the two new ladies, Mrs Perry and Mrs Seymour, found themselves in the middle of a group of women all laughing, with the result that all their shyness and awkwardness disappeared.

Annie finally settled down and sat at the table. Harriet, still laughing, was the first to speak at the meeting.

"If I may address the Madam Chairman, could I ask why she is still wearing her kitchen apron, with a big streak of gravy on the skirt, while taking this meeting?" There was renewed general laughter, as Annie became aware of what she was wearing. She joined in the general laughter, looking comically down at her apron. It was at that moment that her hair fell down at the back.

Pinning up her hair with a bobby pin between her teeth, she said: "Now the newcomers see me in my true light. There is no use me pretending to be anything I'm not, for I'm so easily found out. Now the first item on the agenda is to move a motion that we forget about the 'Mrs' bit, and that we simply welcome our new neighbours, and call them Elise and Cassandra."

"Motion carried," everyone called out together. Annie then abandoned the pretence of conducting a formal meeting and stated their reasons for coming together and asking everyone for their suggestions.

"It's time to try some new things for our Occupational Therapy activities," she concluded. "Florence Armitage made a suggestion which I'll speak of later, but let's put our heads together and try to think of totally different things to do down at the Hospital; doesn't matter how crazy they sound; we can easily scrap something if it doesn't work. Now, you'll have to excuse me for a minute or two, Hannah has told me I have to see Inspector Peters – he's in the next room – only for a moment or two, so Harriet will lead the discussion. Someone, perhaps you … Cassandra … will take a few notes – use the pad on the table – so we don't forget. I won't be long."

Annie hurried into the room where the police were meeting and was talking as she entered the door "… and I don't know, what with the cat dying and with that mother, what the poor girl is going to do now, but that's just what you would expect, with a mother and father like … and." she smiled at the first young policeman, "Constable Watkins soon to be a member of our village; when are the bans being announced I'd like to know? I only said to Mr Tanby the other day, it's time we had someone – a nice widow woman, with a private income – to marry Constable Potts and he could then become part of the anti-freeze campaign – which to my mind is so dangerous, being so deadly – but he's married already."

Annie had reached the Inspector and shaking his hand vigorously greeted the men. "I hope Constable Manders your arm is healed; that dreadful woman – my relative, God rest her soul, nearly got you, didn't she? – And … Sergeant Pierce, I think you've put on weight – most probably the Brawn I taught you."

Turning to the inspector, Annie continued: "Now, you'll have to be quick, I can't leave the ladies for long. Now, do you want to know who killed Jean? Just ask me if you're in difficulties, but I don't think it's that; Hannah said something about crosswords. Why on earth are you policemen sitting around doing crosswords, when we have a killer on the loose? It's beyond me... Inspector?"

"Please sit down, Mrs Watson ... thank you. If I may just ask you to be *quiet* for a moment I'll tell you what I want. I want to read out a list of words to you. They refer to black market goods. I want you to try to tell me what they represent. Clear?"

"Perfectly, Inspector. Off you go."

"Bed-socks?"

"Potatoes."

"Slippery stuff?"

"Could be butter but no, that would require freezing; it'll be honey or golden syrup."

"Billiard balls?"

"Eggs."

"Contained cows?" Annie started to laugh. "That's easy – as well as funny, Tinned Beef."

"4,000 Passes, all rides?"

"My goodness, 4,000! They're *coupons*, of course, all different kinds: food coupons, clothing coupons, you name it – I'll have some, if there are any going free."

"Mechanical starters?"

"You mean you men didn't know that one? Really! All cars need petrol to get them started. It's gallons of petrol."

The men were staring at Annie with amazement. Peters started to laugh. Annie stood up. "Now is there any other little matter you need help with?" she asked with an innocent, deadpan face, her eyebrows arched enquiringly.

"Well, there is as a matter of fact," Peter smiled. "If you were trying to work out the people who live in this area and you only had their initials, would you have any trouble if the initials were OE?"

"OE? Which one? Oh, of *course* ... But, just wait a minute ... Are these initials suspects in the murder?"

"Could be, I'm not really sure yet," admitted Peters.

Annie looked troubled; her brain working feverishly. Should she say something or not? It would only be a guess. No … better to say nothing, than to falsely implicate a person who could be totally innocent. She made a sudden decision.

"No, I'm very sorry, I can't help you there," Annie spoke slowly, and decisively, all laughter gone.

"No matter, we'll find out sooner or later. Thank you Mrs Watson."

Annie tried to return to her light hearted manner. "Remember, Inspector, Jean Harris was a very attractive girl; there wouldn't have been a man in the district who hadn't noticed her. I bought Sam a tomahawk for a birthday gift the other week, just as a reminder of what he'd face if he went to the pub when she was there." Annie waved to the group and hurried from the room to go back to her meeting. A moment later, her head came back round the door. This time she spoke seriously.

"Inspector, there is a policewoman here, a Sergeant Adams, waiting to see you."

After Annie had disappeared again, Inspector Peters swore. "She knew instantly who OE was! And what did she mean, '*which* one?' Does that mean we have two in the village? Who the hell can it be?" He looked up, and then stood. "Come in Sergeant Adams."

FIFTY

Inspector Peters introduced the policewoman to the rest of the men. Sergeant Adams was a sensible looking, comfortable type of woman in her mid-forties with short brown hair going grey who filled her uniform without pretence. She had a clear, somewhat intimidating, no-nonsense manner that she found to her advantage in dealing with the cases that had come to be considered her department. Adams' superior officer, Inspector Jones, had driven her to the pub. He had then returned to The Junction Police Station.

"You are very welcome, Sergeant," Peters said. "Please just sit for a moment and I'll explain the situation – it's not as simple as it sounds."

"It never is, Inspector," replied the woman quietly, seating herself on the spare chair.

"You see," continued Peters, "the situation at the Darcy house appears pretty grim from my sergeant and my constable's reports, but I need access to the father of that family for investigation on two serious charges, one of which is murder."

"Oh dear!" the woman's face indicated her understanding of the difficulty. "So you don't want me hauling him off, when you need him for questioning? Is that it?"

"In a nutshell," smiled Peters. "Could I suggest a compromise? You take Constable Watkins with you for protection; do what you have to do, then, if charges are to be laid, arrange with Watkins for transport back to The Junction Police Station.

"But," Peters continued. "Could I ask a favour? If arrests are to be made, you permit me to retain the father, Alan Darcy, for questioning on a black marketing charge? I'll then keep him at Tavistock police station, where he will be available for questioning by your team, at any time you need him and by me, on the murder charge, which I may be bringing against him. I'll clear that with your Superior, at the Junction, Inspector Jones, if that's all right with you?"

"Sounds a very sensible solution to the problem," The woman stood up. "Must be a charming family. Come on Constable, let's go." Watkins hurriedly opened the door and followed the policewoman out of the room.

Peters sighed. "Now, men, let's get our work sorted out for today."

FIFTY-ONE

The ladies' meeting was in full swing when Annie returned to the room. She left Harriet McKenzie at the table and sat with the other women in chairs haphazardly arranged around the table. Annie listened to her oldest friend, Nan Brady, the dance pianist, as she made a suggestion.

"I've noticed," Nan remarked, smoothing her neat grey hair with her supple elderly fingers which had provided her with a living for the past thirty years, "when Annie does her final fifteen minutes dancing class – and every soldier joins in – the singing is really very good, surprising really. There are some very good voices in the group at the Hospital at the moment."

"Are you thinking of a choir of some sort, Mrs Brady?" asked Elise Seymour timidly.

"It's Nan, dear, not *Mrs* Brady, we're neighbours. No, not a choir – though, that's a possibility. I was thinking more of short Barber-shop quartets – that kind of thing."

"In four parts, Mrs ...er ... Nan?" Nan Brady was no fool. She could see where the newcomer's questions were going.

"Yes, that sort of thing. Now, I suspect you have a pretty good soprano voice Elise. The choir at Mr Norman's church has a fine choir now; are you in it by any chance?"

Elise blushed. "Yes, I am, and ... er ... I love singing. I always have."

"Right," Harriet decided. "We've got a singer and we have the most wonderful pianist we're ever likely to get, so quartets are definitely in. What do you say, Annie?"

"I don't see why we can't have both; choir and quartets. See how simple harmonies go first, Nan, and then we'll go from there." She turned to face Mrs Seymour. 'Elise, have you ever taught or conducted a choir?"

"Only very small ones, Annie," shyly admitted the woman, who ever since she discovered the woman she most wanted to impress, wore an old apron, absentmindedly, to a village meeting, had begun to realise that she was being accepted by her neighbours and that they weren't at all frightening.

For the first time in her life Elise was relaxed in the company of others and, to her amazement, also realised that she was enjoying being part of this community effort – she was just one of them! Elise also understood another truth: although all the women spoke well, used correct grammar and were all well-educated, they were, basically, just like her: a woman with all the trials and tribulations that every woman has to face.

Elise knew now they had definitely made the right decision in coming to this place; she could really be at home here. With a grateful ear she listened to Nan speaking.

"Small ones require just as much attention and training as huge ones," Nan declared. "I think possibly more so: in a big choir if you make a mistake, usually no one really notices; that doesn't happen in a small group. If you make a bad mistake there, it's a disaster."

Annie spoke up. "Now, Florence Armitage had a suggestion," Annie then told of Florence's idea of a short concert, featuring songs, skits, anything they could think up with the emphasis on amusement and laughter.

Cassandra who had spoken little so far, brightened up. "Oh, perhaps I could help there. I'll have to get someone to mind the kids, but Mrs …I'm sorry; Nan said, that perhaps her Norah, would be glad to do so." She took another breath, "I actually was in the university Dramatic Society and my husband, Ron, directed our productions. That's how we met."

"Oh, the talent we have in our famous village now!" cried Annie in delight. Her eyes caught the doctor's wife. "And, of course, Thelma Kemp, you'd be absolutely perfect on the stage. So, no argument, dear, you're going to be a star!" Thelma looked startled, then laughingly agreed. "Right," continued Annie, "we'll definitely have to sort that out; I'll be the villain as usual." This set off a burst of giggling. However, Annie noticed that Laura Hennessy was looking a little left out, as was Hannah Kelly. "But, we have a serious problem."

"What is it, Annie?" asked Harriet, alerted.

"Well, we have new activities suggested and they're damn good ones, but we cannot just drop the ones we've already got established. Some of the boys are incredibly interested in the things they've made with string. The string bags for shopping are doing well in the Red Cross shop at The Junction, aren't they Hannah?"

"They certainly are, also the hammocks."

"Well, they must continue. Hannah, could you and Laura, and perhaps, Harriet ..." she looked swiftly at her friend, who understanding the message, gave a slight nod, "keep up the French knitting, the string work on the bags, and the hammocks?" The three women nodded happily. Annie was aware that Susan Cerney was left without a task.

"Susan, of course," Annie continued, "will be needed for the stage work; we need a beautiful young girl as the heroine."

"Annie, I couldn't!" stammered the young mother of two children, her cheeks flushing prettily.

Whatever Annie was about to answer was interrupted by a loud knock on the door. Betty Johnson came into the room looking flustered.

"Excuse me, ladies. Mrs Kemp and Mrs Watson, you are desperately needed at Mrs Armitage's house; she's gone into labour." There were gasps from around the room. Betty went on. "Mrs Watson, your husband is with her – apparently Dr Kemp had to take an urgent home sick call – and the two young girls with Florence, are frantic. Mr Watson said to tell you, Mrs Watson, to hurry up as he needs help to get the woman down to the Convalescent Hospital to Dr Waters."

Thelma and Annie jumped to their feet. Making for the door, Annie called over her shoulder: "Harriet, arrange it any way you like; make sure everyone knows what their job is for next Tuesday. Put me down for anything; I don't care what it is." Turning to Thelma, Annie charged out the door. "Come on Thelma, let's run. My poor Sam will be a nervous wreck waiting with poor Florrie." The two middle aged women ran from the hotel, knowing that they would both be needed urgently; Florrie would probably be terrified now, at last – after all the waiting – *it was finally happening.*

FIFTY-TWO

Inspector Peters was again interrupted as he was about to allocate the work for his men. Tim Johnson came in carrying an envelope.

"Sorry to interrupt, Inspector, this note was handed in. Ron Perry paid a kid sixpence to deliver this to you; apparently Perry said it was important you should know of it."

Peters thanked the publican and when he had left the room, opened the envelope. "Just as I expected, men, another blackmail letter. I think it's possible that just about every man who comes to the pub received one."

"Which makes it very dangerous for the blackmailer, doesn't it, sir – with someone, he's bound to be right," Pierce said vaguely, as he studied the letter. "Inspector, there's something wrong with this letter … it's beautifully written …" His forehead wrinkled in thought. "Yes, something's not right …"

"You're an observant man, Sergeant," Peters observed. "Yes, it's definitely odd – I've never seen a blackmailing letter written in this particular way – it's out of character, somehow. Let's leave it for the moment. Now, I think we've agreed that everyone involved in the black market gang, or with Jean, is also a suspect in the murder, so I think we have to get them all here to be formally interviewed. Now Pierce, you take Manders with you and collect Jerry Seymour, Alan Darcy – just check out how the policewoman Adams is doing at that place with Constable Watkins – Dan Kelly and the boy Otto Eckhard.

"With the Eckhard boy, Pierce, remember you must ask one of the parents to come with the boy; he's under age. For the others, just take it for granted that they have received one of these letters; ask for it as if you know they have received it." Peters then looked at his old friend.

"Constable Potts, I want you to bring in for questioning our villainous friend, Bert Liveridge, Toby Moore and Ron Perry. What do you think about Alf Cookson, Constable? Think he'll be able to come or not?"

"Well, I haven't seen him this morning, sir, but from what I saw last night, I would think definitely not." Potts scratched his head. "I know you can't play favourites in our game, sir, but … Alf! According to that wretched girl's accounts he only received a measly £20 and all he spent it on was a pathetic carpet square … I mean, compared to the others …"

"I understand, perfectly, Constable; it goes without saying that I agree with you. Let's just take it slowly shall we? If possible, when you bring the others in to me, you could slip in there and have a private chat, with either Alf or his wife – try to find out just how much Alf knew of the whole business … you know the drill."

Potts looked relieved and got up to leave. "And, you, sir, will you still be here at the pub?"

"Most probably. If not, just wait for me. I want to have a quick word with Reg Cerney. He's a shrewd judge of character and I'm unsure if he came to the pub that night or not. I'll slip up to the forge and see him for a moment, then hurry back here. I hear the women breaking up their meeting next door, so I'll grab the chance to speak to them as well. So, off you go to catch the villains and I'll chat up the fair sex.

"Ah! The perks of office!" The men dutifully laughed and set off, carefully wrapping scarves around their necks and buttoning their official overcoats; it was another cold winter's day and the wind was, once again, freezing.

FIFTY-THREE

Policewoman Adams and Constable Watkins heard the Darcys in full voice before they turned the corner into Quarry Lane. Apparently a terrible row was in progress, with much screaming. The policewoman paused a moment and then shocked Watkins, by swearing.

"Bloody hell! This is going to be fun! Have you got your truncheon handy, Constable? Right, in we go and no pussy-footing about either; we're the tough guys remember? Right, off we go."

Watkins – used to the politeness of Peters – was astonished at Sergeant Adams' manner. However, he had no option but to follow the policewoman as she ran through the gate and in the open door, shouting in a loud voice: "Police raid, Police raid, all lie on the floor!" The woman had her truncheon in her hand and brandished it threatening.

There was stunned silence, the five figures standing as statues in their shock. Adams didn't give them time to recover. "You," she shouted to Alan Darcy, "do as I told you. Down on the floor."

"Like bloody hell, I will," he angrily replied and advanced on the policewoman. Watkins prepared to intervene, when he found it wasn't necessary. Adams had taken the man's hand as he advanced; suddenly, Mr Darcy went over the woman's shoulder to crash down on the floor.

"That's a good boy; down on the floor, just as I said." Adams turned to the wife still standing with her mouth wide open. "Close your mouth, you look disgusting. Sit on that chair there and do not move." She looked for the first time at the children; saw with surprise that the eldest girl – looked about thirteen or fourteen – was cuddling a dead cat in her arms, her face tragic; she was crying helplessly.

Adams also noted a lout of a boy about twelve, who looked at the moment as if he was about to wet his pants, then finally at a small child – seemed about four – who, to her disgust, was still wearing a nappy which desperately needed changing. All the children were marked with the clear signs of malnutrition, neglect and brutal treatment. The sergeant's voice softened. She looked at the girl.

"Tell me your name and the name of your cat which you loved."

Buffy raised swollen, red, surprised eyes to the policewoman's face. "I'm Buffy, and this was my baby, Mingy. They've killed my cat; the only thing I loved on earth; they've killed it. I wish they'd kill each other and be finished with it. With Mingy gone, now, I've got nothing ..." the child burst again into scalding tears.

"Bloody filthy flea-ridden pest," harangued the woman. "Didn't kill it, but I often wanted to. Disease ridden menace – good riddance I say."

"Hold your peace, you despicable apology for a mother," demanded Adams, "this is a police raid so you'll only speak when you're spoken to, or I'll arrest you."

"You'll what?" gasped Sheila Darcy.

The policewoman turned to Buffy. "Now, I want to talk to you and the younger children. I cannot call you, Buffy – it's the name of a dog. What is your real name?"

"Rosemary," was the muffled answer.

"Well, Rosemary, pick up the youngest child, bring him here to me, and get a clean nappy."

"I don't know if we have any more that are dry. I washed some this morning."

"*You* washed them? Good! Write that down Constable. See if you can find one anyhow, dear." Rosemary put her cat down on a chair and did as she was told. She soon came back with a dry napkin of a grey-brown colour. The policewoman thanked her and taking the little child's hand she took the child over to its mother and grabbing the woman's hair wrenched her head back until she shrieked. "Now, you," said the Sergeant softly, "will wash and clean your child and put on him a clean nappy."

Adams went across to stand with Rosemary. "Now, we've got to give your baby a proper burial. What was its name again?"

"Mingy."

"Well, Constable Watkins here is an expert at funerals. You will take him out to the front and find a suitable spot and," she turned swiftly to the father still lying on the floor. "You! Get up! Get a spade and give it to the constable; if it isn't done within two minutes, I'll take you with your charming wife back to the station."

She looked at the constable and nodded. He took the girl with her cat gently out the front door and, having received the spade from the father, began the burial of Mingy with all the solemnity and seriousness he could muster, ad lib.

Rosemary cried throughout, but now it was not the desperate, despairing crying that it had been before. When the impromptu service was over, Watkins found two pieces of broken fence palings and fashioned a rough cross which he ceremoniously, and solemnly, erected over the grave.

Back inside, Sergeant Adams had questioned both mother and father and inspecting the cupboards, found that there was virtually nothing in the house to eat; that the children had had no breakfast but, as the questioning continued, she decided that the father, Alan Darcy, was in all probability a drunken wastrel, but he had not personally maltreated the children; but Sheila had broken every rule in the book.

While Watkins was engaged outside with the funeral, Sergeant

Adams took great pleasure in forcing Sheila to clean and actually scrub the kitchen – floor as well as walls. She made Alan Darcy light the copper and prepare the huge mound of washing. Watkins, his funeral over, came back inside the house with Rosemary. The sergeant was talking to Alan Darcy.

"You'll need to know how to do it, Mr Darcy," she informed him, "for I'm arresting your wife for criminal neglect; also for placing the eldest child in a situation that is tantamount to being in moral danger. I'll arrange for the collection of the three children by the proper authorities today. For the moment, I am not going to charge you – in relation to the family situation – but Inspector Peters demands that you go with Constable Watkins to be questioned, at the pub, on another matter entirely. Isn't that the case, Constable Watkins?"

"It is, Sergeant, and if you are ready, Mr Darcy, I'll take you in now."

"What! You're joking! What the bloody hell is going on ... just because a silly letter ..." Watkins was quick to seize on this remark.

"And that reminds me, Mr Darcy, the inspector had instructed me to take the letter you received, from you, by force, if necessary. But, after your little attempt to attack the sergeant here, I might remind you that we both trained at the same institution." He looked at the sergeant; she nodded. "Shall we go, then?" Darcy, taking the letter out of his pocket held it out to Watkins who led the bewildered man out to the police car and left the policewoman to supervise Sheila Darcy doing the washing at the tubs.

Sheila's face was scarlet with fury, Adams' face with complete satisfaction. She sat on a low stool, holding the hand of the girl, Rosemary, with the little boy, Harry, on her knee. Oliver was obliged to sit still at the kitchen table and do a jigsaw, which this resourceful policewoman had taken from her uniform pocket. He was not happy.

FIFTY-FOUR

Alexander Seymour was bored. Yesterday had been fun, so had last night. After his early rising to attend to the Darcy cat, Alex was also sleepy. He had taken his new money to the shop – it was only three doors away, next to the empty fish shop – and tried to buy some things. Unfortunately there were not very exciting things on the shelves that interested him. However, he did see a very expensive, leather-bound note book and bought it, so surprising Mrs Eckhard, she looked at the child over the top of her spectacles.

Alex was aware of her suspicions, but the shop keeper said nothing. After all, a sale of a notebook, that no one wanted, at the princely price of five shillings, was not something to be sniffed at. Alex bought some hard-boiled sweets which he hated, and a bar of chocolate which was hideously expensive, then, after eating the entire block in one go, he discovered was not very nice either.

After his mother came back from the pub meeting of the ladies, she was in a very happy mood and attempted to tell her pride and joy all about it. Alex was not interested in a lot of sick soldiers.

"Why don't they go back to the war," he asked. "We're supposed to be in real trouble aren't we? Australia, I mean – a lot of baloney I think. The Japs could never win."

"I'm sorry to say, Alexander," protested his mother, "but there is a distinct possibility that they will, unless the Americans can keep up the wonderful work they are doing in the Pacific – that's where we live, dear, in the Pacific region."

"Oh, for Pete's sake, I know that! I'm not a kid. I'm a very clever young man and when I am in charge of the war, we'll see a big change I can tell you. Anyhow, I'm going to lie down …" Elise was immediately concerned.

"Are you ill, Alex? Do you want me to send for the doctor?"

"Aw! Of course I don't want the stupid doctor; he's so old he's useless anyhow."

"That's not true; he's a very clever doctor and his wife is such a nice lady."

"What on earth has that to do with it? She's not the doctor! I'm going to my room."

Back in his bedroom, Alex lay on the bed thinking about his success with the cat. Well, it certainly worked with a cat, would it be as easy with a kid? I wonder if it would work on Jason in the same way. Perhaps later, when tonight's over?

Tonight, he smiled as he anticipated the night; he was going to make a bundle! Alex still felt restless, so decided to see what was happening at the Darcy house. Missing their cat I bet, he grinned. He put on his 'pretend' sorrowful face. How sad! It'd really make you cry, it would! Alex then laughed out loud; the thought of Mingy made him feel better already.

FIFTY-FIVE

As Inspector Peters walked into the forge behind Nan Brady's house, he found Reg Cerney at the anvil, with the fire roaring. A toddler, kept well away from the furnace, wearing a miniature apron and holding a rubber hammer, was banging away on a make-believe anvil at the same time.

Peters had not seen young Ben for ages and was astonished to see the child so advanced, not the slightest bit afraid of the noise of the anvil, or the fire. Reg looked up and stopped his work.

"Ben, looks who's here!" he cried picking up his son in his brawny arms, and stretching out his hand to the policeman. They had been friends for three years now – three terrible years of war and tragedy. Reg looked a little bit stockier than he had been; he now had a settled, satisfied air about him – that of a happy man.

"You're looking wonderful Reg, my boy," Peters greeted his young friend. "As you might expect I've come wanting something. I need your help in this case."

"Another awful one, Inspector. Yet, another young woman. Who will ever forget our first one? Not me, I can tell you."

"Did you know this one, Reg? Know Jean at all well?"

"No, I saw her a couple of times in the pub, but I don't go there much now; perhaps a beer twice a week that's the limit. I've got too much to lose by stupidly wasting money."

"What did you think of her?"

"I suppose what everyone else did; that she was not a good woman; that she was on the make; that she'd use every opportunity she could to further her plans, whatever they were."

"Did she ever approach you, or flirt with you? She certainly did with so many others."

"Yes, she did, when she first came here. She's a type, easily enough recognized. Slap them down thoroughly in the beginning and you're not pestered with them again; which is what I did."

"Reg, are you aware that there was something crook going on between Jean Harris and some of the men? I don't mean hanky panky, I mean activities that could hinder the war effort, harm Australia?"

Reg grew thoughtful. "That's strange you saying that, Inspector. I've known girls who were 'bar-flies', but I did wonder a couple of times, why that girl was flitting from one bloke to the next, every time I happened to see her in the bar. I did wonder, at one time, if she could be giving the men instructions, but I reprimanded myself: thought it was just my wild Irish imagination."

Reg paused. "So, there was something going on, was there?"

"I would say definitely, yes. Now Reg, tell me honestly were you in the pub, or near the pub, Thursday night?"

"Not on your life. That's a night that Nan is *always* home. For some unknown reason, no one has dances, or parties, on Thursday nights. She's always home that night, so Susan, Norah and I try to make something special of those precious nights, when she's *not* working. We call those nights our real family nights."

"You are a good man, Reg Cerney," Peters declared. "Truly Nan Brady should be given a medal after the war. I think playing for dances up to five nights a week for soldiers, year after year, is incredible. She has spent more time in the army than most soldiers." The two men laughed and Peters turned to leave. "Yes, she deserves a medal. Good bye young Ben – you're going to be just like your father, do you know that?"

"God help him then!" laughed Reg.

"No, thank God, Reg, thank God. I see too much of the other sort."

FIFTY-SIX

Constable Potts had no difficulty with either Ron Perry or Toby Moore. Both men came quietly and were obviously ashamed of being seen entering a police car. They nodded briefly to each other, then sat rigidly against the extreme sides of the back seat. Toby Moore handed over the letter immediately he was asked, looking red in the face, while Ron reminded Potts that he had sent his to the inspector earlier that morning.

It was a different matter when Potts came to Bert Liveridge. First of all, Bert refused to come with the policeman; then he utterly denied that he had received a letter at all. Lily Liveridge, hovering in the background, horrified the neighbours would see her husband being taken away in a police car, hurried into their bedroom and handed Potts a crumpled letter, which she had extracted from under the pillow.

"Is this the letter, Constable?" she asked tremulously, "I saw Bert reading it as I came to bed. He wouldn't let me see it ..."

"Don't listen to her! It's a lie! She's always been against me, she has," Bert shouted. He turned to his wife and lifted his hand. Lily cowered back.

That was enough for Potts; he had spent his life sorting out drunks and, with a strong muscled arm, suddenly grabbed Bert by the collar, dragged him out into the street, and threw him into the front seat of the car. The neighbours were out in force, goggling at the spectacle.

Alexander Seymour was in the front row, savouring this wonderful entertainment. Things certainly happened when you lived in Quarry Lane! When Liveridge was safely locked in the car, Potts warned him, if he persisted in his behaviour, he'd have two more charges added to the ones, they already had against him. He also informed him that the inspector was waiting at the pub to officially charge him with a criminal offence, so 'he'd better belt up and shut his trap, or he'd end up with some bruises he didn't expect'.

Potts then politely said, "Good Morning," to Mrs Liveridge, got in the car with his bunch of suspects and drove, quickly and efficiently, back to the pub.

Meanwhile Sergeant Pierce, accompanied by Constable Manders, had had an easier time collecting his suspects. Constable Watkins had already delivered Alan Darcy to the pub, and Dan Kelly and Gerald Seymour came without a murmur. Otto Eckhard, refusing utterly to be accompanied by his mother or father, sat between Manders and Seymour in the back, his face scarlet. Dan sat in the front seat; he and Pierce chatted about the latest war news during the drive back to the pub, where the inspector, back from the forge, was waiting to receive them.

FIFTY-SEVEN

Policewoman Adams looked with satisfaction at the washing, now hanging on the line. She had also organized the three children so that they each had bathed and were now wearing clean, if unironed, clothes. Watkins had helped in just about every task in sorting out the mess of the house, including helping to hang out the washing and was now waiting for orders from the Sergeant.

"Constable Watkins," Adams confided, "I'm in a bit of a quandary here. I've got to take the Darcy woman to The Junction to be charged; she will definitely be kept at least until she comes up before a magistrate Monday morning … but it's the kids. I don't like leaving them with only Rosemary to look after them – especially with that bruiser of a boy, Oliver. Do you know of any woman I could ask to look after them for a day or two, just until I can find a place that will take them?"

"Sergeant, that's not an easy request, given that there are three children. However, I do know an extraordinary woman, Annie Watson, who I think is our only hope. She is often wildly eccentric, but a very compassionate and loving woman. I think she'd take the girl and the young child, Harry. It's the boy, Oliver, who worries me most – just dumping him on her. But we could at least try her."

"Could you go and get her to come and have a look at the situation, do you think?"

"I certainly could," Watkins paused. "I've just had an idea. The local blacksmith, Reg Cerney is a very good man; also a very *strong* man, I was wondering if he would take the older boy and Mrs Watson take the other two?"

"It may not be necessary at all, of course, unless Inspector Peters arrests Alan Darcy. From what he told me and your own report, Rosemary cooks most of the meals that are cooked in this house, so if her father comes back this afternoon, they could stay with him."

"What do you think will happen to the mother? I mean, is she likely to go to goal?"

"No, not for a first offence and one that is the least of the categories I deal with. She'll come up before the magistrate on Monday morning; she'll be told off, get a fine and a warning, then be put on a register for regular visits from the Social Worker. I expect she'll be back home Monday afternoon."

Watkins felt relieved. "Well, if Inspector Peters let Darcy come home we're all right?"

"That's it. However, just in case circumstances change and Darcy doesn't come home, I must have a plan for the children. So, if you would see the Watson lady and see whether she would consider it, as only a possible contingency, then we've done all we can do."

The policewoman sighed. "Oh, all the odds and ends you have to think of and investigate, whenever you try to fix a situation."

"That's what my inspector says about the murder investigations we do. Most of the routine work is boring and useless in the long run, but simply has to be done to get to the truth."

"Peters is a good man; you're lucky to have him. Right, off you go to Mrs Watson and, if she's free, bring her here. If that works out, I'll see the blacksmith myself." The policewoman watched as Watkins left the house and then turned to Rosemary. "Now, dear, we're going to introduce young Harry to the potty; it's high time he was out of nappies – it's disgusting. Let's make a start anyway."

Policewoman Ruby Adams was a remarkably practical woman.

FIFTY-EIGHT

Major Ted Waters peeled off his rubber gloves, threw them into the bin and scrubbed his hands. He spoke over his shoulder.

"There you are, Mrs Armitage, a beautiful little son and not so little either; he's going to be a big man. It was one of the quickest deliveries I've ever seen. I think you could have handled it yourself; there was so little for me to do. I am so glad for you."

Florence looking exhausted, flushed and sweaty, stared at the bundle in her arms with an air of bewilderment. "It doesn't seem possible, Doctor, does it? One minute you're in agony; the next, you're holding a new life in your arms." Florence raised her beautiful eyes to the doctor. "I cannot thank you enough, Dr Waters. When I discovered Dr Kemp was away on a case I panicked; thank God, you let me come here."

"I think we'll have to change our notice board," joked the doctor, "as you know that's the second birth that's occurred here – very odd when you come to think of it; it's a Hospital for *male* soldiers." He laughed and turned to the Theatre sister.

"And you, Sister Rumpit, officiated at both births!" He smiled. "Thank you again, Sister, you were splendid." Rumpit flushed with the compliment and began to sponge Florence's face and neck. Florence looked questioning at the nursing sister, "Sister, is he ...?" Sister Rumpit understood instantly.

"He's absolutely perfect, dear; a wonderfully healthy, perfectly formed baby boy; nothing to worry about at all." The nursing Sister turned to the doctor. "Now, tell me Doctor, are the stupid army authorities going to permit the husband, Captain Armitage – whom I remember very well – to come and see his son and heir?" Dr Waters turned to his patient.

"Mrs Armitage, I've contacted the Captain's Colonel and as Stephen's not far away, they are giving him a couple of days' leave, so he should be here very soon. But you have a couple of very anxious visitors waiting outside for their first peep of the infant. Are mother and child both respectable, Sister? If so, let the visitors come in."

Soon the bed was surrounded, first with Annie and Thelma, then with most of the ladies from the group in the pub. Annie was crying and holding fast to Florence's hand. "You did it, Florrie, you did it! Oh, thank God, it all went well. I'll phone Mother Benedicta as soon as I get home."

Annie then stepped back, controlling herself and said with mock severity: "Now that you've sorted out that minor problem, Florrie, you can spend the next few hours, pondering on that list of names, I gave you." She gave Florence's hand a final squeeze, and called over her shoulder as she left the room. "God bless you darling girl. I'm off now; you must get some rest. I can't wait to see you back to your elegant figure, with all your fabulous clothes fitting you once again."

FIFTY-NINE

Constable Watkins was still busily engaged in his work with the policewoman, but Pierce, Manders and Potts were back in the pub having brought in the men for questioning. Peters had demanded the suspects be seated at a distance from each other around the bar room with Potts keeping an eye on them – to prevent any collusion.

The Inspector had a quick briefing with his men in the hall of the pub.

"Look, as far as I can determine, we can eliminate Dan Kelly, Ron Perry and Liveridge from the murder; and of those, only Bert Liveridge is seriously involved in the black market gang. However, the murder is our first priority, so let's get rid of Kelly and Perry quickly. Then we'll deal with Liveridge and the rest of those involved in the black market gang. I'm going to arrest Liveridge and send him off to the station – I'm sorry, but he'll go to goal, the silly old chap – then, I have to deal with that German boy.

"I'll have to be careful, with him being a minor; we'll handle him separately. I shall keep the other suspects, for *both* crimes free, for the moment – the boy's only a 'possible' for the murder. If I'm right, the others will be worrying themselves sick with Liveridge in goal – they know how he'll crack under any pressure – we might get the truth out of them then. OK?" The policemen nodded.

As Peters was leaving the group of men, he remembered Alf Cookson. Going back to Potts he asked him quietly about the man.

"I asked, sir," Potts answered, "and he still has not uttered a word. Mrs Cookson looks nearly dead with worry; apparently the doctor is still not certain whether it's a stroke or not." Potts shook his head. "Anyway as far as we're concerned, there's no chance of him being fit for any questioning."

Peters listened intently. He then leant over Potts so that no one else could hear him. "Potts, do you think you could get that blasted carpet away from the house? What the hell could we do with it? Any ideas? It's really the only evidence that Alf benefited from the gang activity. If that was gone, it would be hard to prove he had any involvement." He smiled. "And do you know, I think I inadvertently erased his name from the list of amounts of money in the book." Potts' face indicated his understanding. Peters started to leave as Potts spoke.

"Leave it to me, sir. I'll get rid of the damn thing; the charity shops are always looking for good furnishings. Ada Cookson is a sensible and good woman; I'll have a word with her, before I go home. I'll deal with it, sir ... and sir," Peters turned back to his Constable, his eyes raised questioningly, "thank you."

Peters smiled, then looking at the group of suspects, called loudly, his voice coldly officious: "Dan Kelly! Come with me."

SIXTY

Telephone call from Penelope McKenzie to her mother Annie Watson.

"Mum? ... Glad I caught you; I have some news for you. Firstly, tell me are you well? ... Yes, it *is* bad news, I'm sorry ... *Please*, Mum, just keep quiet will you; this is important, no dramatics please ... I will... *when you are quiet*. I'll tell you then, *not* before.

"That's better ... Now, George and I will be coming to stay with George's parents tonight, until Monday morning ... Yes, at the McKenzie house, not with you ... No, you see, dear, your house is just not grand enough now that George is such an important person ... Mum, I'm *joking*! Really! For the love of Mike! Well, if you *must* know, the police ordered it ...Yes I thought that would stop you. *Now* will you listen?

"We had a bomb planted in our house ... Mum? *Mum*? *MUM*? Are you still there? I had to hold the receiver away from my ear with that shrieking ... Well, it's because things have hotted up ... No, neither George nor I were hurt, but the house is a wreck; the poor security guard who impersonates George, was badly hurt; he may not live ... Oh, I forgot, I hadn't told you about that...

"No matter... the main thing is that the police won't take any more responsibility for us, unless we move to somewhere safer and they think that Bexford North *might* be safer until the trial is over ... If that proves dangerous to Harriet and George, the police are going to insist that my George stays in his Chambers in the city, under guard, then it will only be me living at the McKenzie house …

"How am I? Well, considering all that has happened since this trial began, I think I'm coping rather well … Yes, of course I'm taking every precaution I can … Anyhow, one good thing, Mum, we'll have a chance to see you tomorrow … George will be disguised a little, so don't carry on about it; he will be coming with you and the Cerney crowd, to Mass on Sunday up at the Wembley Hospital chapel … Yes, well, the police thought that one up.

"As George isn't a Catholic, they thought the disguise would be even better if he's seen going to a Catholic Church on a Sunday … That's all, Mum … Mum … Oh, *Mum* … I … No! … Nothing, Mum … just a sniffle … no, I'm *not* … crying … really and truly … must go … something in my eye... Bye, Mum."

SIXTY-ONE

Dan Kelly was puzzled as he entered the small parlour where Inspector Peters and Sergeant Pierce were waiting for him. He saw Constable Manders sitting to the side with his notebook ready on his knee.

"I don't understand, Inspector," Dan began, "I thought we had our talk earlier today up at the farm."

"We did, Dan," replied Peters. "Just sit down; I promise you I'll not keep you long." The Inspector referred to his notes.

"Now, you said you had a quarrel with Bianca, pretended to flirt with Jean before she left the pub, then Bianca left you in anger. You hurried out after her and the last you saw of Jean, she was standing near the water-trough. Is that correct?"

"Yes, Inspector."

"Did you go straight home?"

"Yes."

"What time did you get in, do you know?"

"Not sure, Mum and Sally were listening to the wireless on the ABC; some play or something. It was just finishing if that's any help. I think it was about half past eight o'clock – about that anyhow.

"I would have stayed longer listening to the music that was playing on the wireless after the play – it was Tommy Dorsey and his orchestra; I like him – but I was still angry and just wanted to get to my room – there's not much privacy at home."

"Right. Well, Dan, we have an unimpeachable witness who actually saw Jean Harris alive at half past nine o'clock, so you're in the clear if what you say is true, and after our talk this morning, I see no reason to doubt you."

He shifted in his chair. "Dan, you can go home; we won't be bothering you again, unless something unforseen comes up." Peters stood up and held out his hand. Kelly, surprised, shook his hand, nodded to the other men and left the room. Peters noticed the surprised look on his sergeant's face.

Peters apologized to his colleagues. "I'm sorry, men, I realise now I had forgotten to tell you. Mrs Watson told me she heard Jean talking near the water-trough, well and truly alive, at half past nine o'clock. She told me when she first came to see the dead body in the trough. I thought you knew."

"That's cleared up one mystery for me," declared Pierce. "I was wondering how on earth you were so definite about the time of the murder. Did Mrs Watson have any idea who was with Jean?"

"I'm not sure; she plays the cards close to her chest when she wants to. I think she actually did know, or had a shrewd idea. Anyhow she changed the subject quickly, Sergeant. Right, Manders, next one: Ron Perry."

The interview with Ron Perry took exactly four minutes. Peters told the man to remain standing.

"Listen to me carefully, Mr Perry," the inspector spoke sternly. "I am giving you a chance you don't really deserve. I am taking into consideration that you came to us of your own accord to tell us of your involvement with Jean Harris. Secondly, you sent me the blackmailing letter soon after I arrived here this morning.

"Apart from that, you have nothing whatsoever to be pleased about. You have betrayed your wife and your four wonderful children. You have been played for a fool by a designing young female; you have disgraced your important position by turning a blind eye to something evil you suspected was going on; finally, you have been found disloyal to the very fine Minister of the Crown that you represent. If he knew of your behaviour, he would be simply ashamed of you.

"You are a young, very foolish man. I am giving you another chance. Grow up and face your responsibilities – learn to discern good from evil, in your associates. You hold a vital position in regard to the war effort and you hold in your hands the chance of real happiness with your young family. Don't throw that away; it's precious,"

Peters stood up. "Good afternoon." Ron Perry stumbled out of the room, his face scarlet. It was not until he had left the building that he understood what the Inspector had done for him: he was now a free man … he was now *free*!

Back inside the room, Inspector Peters grimaced and, turning to Sergeant Pierce said, "That was the easy one. Now for the drama! Manders, bring in that pestilential nuisance, Bert Liveridge.

SIXTY-TWO

Policewoman Adams stood with Annie Watson in the Darcy kitchen. She had brought the children in for Annie to see and had sent them to the front room which had been tidied. The children sat there rigidly waiting to hear their fate. Mrs Darcy was ordered to sit on a kitchen chair; she was furious.

"Mrs Watson," she demanded, "can't you stop this madwoman? They've taken off my husband who was brutally handled by this female Amazon; now she's taking my children away from me."

"Don't answer her, Mrs Watson," ordered the Sergeant. "She will be taken to The Junction to the cells, then brought up before the magistrate on Monday morning where she will be charged with serious child neglect and exposing her oldest child to moral danger."

Annie felt wretched. She understood how she would feel if her own children were being taken away, yet she knew that there must have been just cause for the police to have acted as they had.

But take the children to her place? Dear God, with all the trouble now with Penny and her husband? How could she possibly manage? What would Sam say if she calmly came home with three kids? The sergeant led Annie to the front room.

She looked at the eldest child, who refused to meet her eye, but stared at her feet. Annie noted the poor, pitifully thin cardigan, the cold house without even a fire; the blue fingers of the little boy whose big eyes were staring at this stranger.

Dear God, how can I *not* do it? Annie then looked closely at the boy, Oliver. She had encountered Oliver before and had a broken window to remember him by. No, I'm sorry God, but I can't take Oliver; I couldn't manage him; Sam wouldn't be happy to leave him in the house without supervision. Yet, how terrible to be separated from your brother and sister!

Oh, this is too hard a decision to make; too much to have to cope with – as well as Penny's situation.

"Sergeant, I don't think I can do it," she said at last. "It's not that I don't want to; I don't think I can manage." She lowered her voice. "It's the boy; I couldn't manage the boy."

"Constable Watkins had an idea about the blacksmith, Mr Cerney. What do you think?"

"Well, Reg would manage him all right, there's no doubt about that, but it's a full house already – and with little children. Oh, dear, I'm sorry; Reg will have to answer for himself. I cannot take on that responsibility."

The sergeant shrugged. "Well, I really do understand. They'll just have to come with me. The Children's Home for the Homeless and Neglected will just have to make room for them, even though they're bulging at the seams already. They can sleep on the floor."

"Over my dead body!" Annie shouted angrily. "Rosemary, Harry, come here." The two children came towards her and Annie picked up the little boy and put her arm around Rosemary. "Oliver, you come with me, too. Your dad will most probably be home – from what the sergeant said, but if he isn't, I'll take all of you to stay with me." Annie found the policewoman looking at her, smiling.

"Thank you Mrs Watson. I'll get your phone number from the constable, and be in touch with you, if the children are to come to you. The constable will drive you back home now."

Back in the car, Annie and Constable Watkins looked wryly at each other. "Well, Constable, if you ring me later and tell me that I'm to take the kids, what the hell is Sam going to say to me when

I arrive home with a new family? I don't think he'll be pleased, do you?"

Watkins smiled, shook his head and pursed his lips; it was just as well Sam Watson was such an easy going chap – he was thinking most blokes would be livid – he knew he would.

The Darcy house being on the corner of Tully Road and Quarry Lane made it easy for Alexander Seymour, lingering, out of sight, near the open front door of the house to listen intently to all that had been said.

He rubbed his hand together with delight: Crikey, there I was thinking it was a boring day! It gets better and better! The kids' old woman's going to goal, and the old man is probably there already! Wait till I tell everyone about this!

SIXTY-THREE

Back at the pub, Bert Liveridge sat uneasily in front of the policemen. There was silence in the room which reduced Bert, in spite of the cold day, to break out in a sweat.

Manders!"

"Sir."

"Go to the office and ring for the Paddy Wagon. Tell them we have one man for the cells. He is to be charged under the Emergency Wartime Powers Act, with being an active member of a black market gang operating here in Bexford North. He has consorted freely with the main members of the gang, benefited to the extent of hundreds of pounds, the evidence is clearly to be seen in his house and he has made false declarations to an officer of the Australian Police Force." Manders left the room.

"Mr Liveridge," Peters continued, "Sergeant Pierce will now read you your rights."

Sergeant Pierce stood up and began reading from his well worn police notebook, only to be interrupted by the inspector.

"Excuse me, Pierce, I think the poor old chap has fainted; he can't hear you. Could you get him a drink of water from the kitchen?"

Twenty minutes later, a badly shaken Bert Liveridge was led, handcuffed, by a different constable through the midst of the other suspects to the waiting wagon. All eyes followed the elderly man, until he was locked inside the vehicle and it had driven away.

Peters rubbed his aching eyes. "Now for the difficult one … I am so tired. Ah, well! Must be done; bring in Mister Eckhard."

The inspector was surprised at his first sight of the young man. Surprised and mentally thrown off balance. Otto was nearly the height of Constable Manders, and possibly even broader in the shoulders. The boy looked twenty, not sixteen. Peters saw the handsome face; the golden hair, the startling blue eyes … and shivered involuntarily.

He was looking at the archetypal 'Aryan' face of Hitler's propaganda machine. This was unnerving; Pierce actually drew in his breath audibly, while his eyes never left the face opposite him.

Rarely was Inspector Peters unsure of himself in interrogations, but now, he was at a loss how to start. Sergeant Pierce, seeing his superior officer in apparent difficulties, and quickly understanding the reason, came to his assistance.

"I have to remind you, Mr Eckhard, that you were offered the opportunity to have one of your parents with you and you deliberately said you would – to quote from what you said," Pierce looked at his notes, "'face the swine alone, or not at all.' Is that correct?"

The boy yawned. "Well, I haven't changed my mind if that's what's bothering you,"

Peters was aware he had to take control quickly. He spoke coldly, but being a decent and scrupulously fair man, was painfully aware of his prejudice. He realised that had the boy not looked so terrifyingly German, he would treat him differently.

"I see. So you regard us as swine. That is interesting, as that expression is used by the Nazis regularly. I was not under the impression, from your splendid parents, that you had leanings in that directions."

"Come off it! You know perfectly well I don't, so don't try any police tricks with me."

"I won't then," Peters answered. "I'll come straight to the point.

Why did you kill the Harris girl?" The boy gasped, his face turned a pasty colour under his golden tan.

Peters went on. "We have evidence that you were intimate with her. What happened, did she throw you over for someone a little more experienced than a mere boy? Someone who was not still carrying his little sandwiches – to eat in the playground?"

Otto blushed scarlet. "How dare you! Who told you about Jean and me? Go on, tell me, I'll punch their heads in; I'm a champion boxer you know."

"Oh yes? I must check up with the instructor at the gym. Which one is it by the way?"

"It's Kell O'Grady's at The Junction; he'll tell you. I work out three times a week and have won my first two fights in the ring. I've also won trophies for shooting."

"Quite the perfect, complete man," Peters calmly responded. "Well, you possibly *could* be, when you reach an age when you have to *shave* everyday. For the moment we'll have to deal with the adolescent *boy* you actually *are*."

Peters sighed wearily. "Tell me, how did you meet Jean Harris?" After the allusion to shaving, the boy was less arrogant, more on his guard.

"She picked me ... I mean *I* picked her up at the Pictures," there was a desperate attempt to regain the cynical, adult, male role he had started with. "She was an easy one; hands all over me after a few minutes, if you know what I mean."

"And she dropped you?"

"What if she did? I had a good time with her."

"You were angry ..."

"What if I was? Wouldn't you be, except you're too old to interest any woman?"

Peters slammed his fist on the table making it rock.

"Look sonny. I've had a very trying day and I have plenty to do before it's over. You will answer my questions in a civil manner; any more smart-arsed answers and I'll run you in. You could easily find yourself in a Juvenile Detention Centre. You wouldn't like that, I'm telling you. You think you're such a big he-man; let me tell you something: the inmates there would eat you for breakfast." Peters turned to his sergeant, his voice contemptuous.

"Ring the station, Sergeant Pierce, and see if the Juvenile Detention officer is on duty this afternoon." Pierce stood up. Otto realised he was treading on very thin ice now, so rushed into speech.

"No, don't do that; I know I've been rude. I'm sorry. I thought it'd be funny, but it isn't. My parents are very good and decent people; they'd die if I ended up in one of those places. My brothers and one sister are in the Armed Forces, too. I know I look like one of Hitler's posters of the 'perfect race' so I thought I'd try to act like one."

"You are a blasted waste of my valuable time with your childish behaviour. I've a good mind to teach you a lesson you won't forget in a hurry; you need a good belting … Now, what the hell is this?"

Tim Johnson had knocked briefly on the door and rushed in.

"Inspector, you have to go immediately to Kelly's farm. Apparently the parents of the dead girl have turned up; they have openly accused Dan of the murder of their daughter; now Mrs Harris is sporting a very bad black eye from Mrs Kelly's fist."

"Dear God in Heaven! How much more?" exclaimed Peters. "Thank you Tim. Mr Eckhard you may go. I'll be in touch with you again, possibly many times; you are a definite suspect in the murder of Jean Harris." Peters raised his voice. "Out! Now! Jump to it!"

The inspector waited until the boy had scurried from the room; he then turned to the sergeant. "Pierce, take the other suspects, just get down the times they left the pub – as far as they remember – did they see Jean Harris outside, did they speak to her, did they go straight home, have they anyone who can alibi their stories … you know what we want. Then let them go home, but I want to have a meeting with our men here before we leave today." He stood up. "I'm sorry Pierce, but I'll have to take Manders with me. OK?

"Right, sir, off you go. A black eye, eh? I wouldn't care to get a black eye from Mrs Kelly – she'd pack a powerful punch."

SIXTY-FOUR

Brian and Beryl Harris had arrived at Hannah Kelly's house complete with suitcases intending to stay, not mincing words about it either. They were in a vile mood, not from the sad occurrence of their daughter's tragic death, but because they had been forced to miss the day's horse races.

Their neighbours had carried on so much that they had no alternative, in order to save face, than to pack and travel the long distance from Newcastle to Bexford North. To add to their irritation, they had to wait a full hour for the bus and, when it had finally arrived at the station, found that the driver, Jim Fellows, had received their complaints about slack service, with complete indifference.

They also expressed their outrage at the fare and were refused entry until they had stumped up the one shilling and sixpence for the two tickets.

Arriving at Hannah's house they had hammered loudly on the door until it had been thrown open with such force, that it knocked the short, obese woman off her feet, and sent her hat flying.

Brian Harris had immediately informed Hannah that they would sue for assault, declaring that it was easy to see that the son, Daniel the murderer, must be the image of his mother. Beryl Harris, picking herself up from the path and patting herself down, pulled her pink straw on, after checking it carefully to see that it was not damaged.

She then proceeded to say what she thought of the reception

they had received. Apparently that was when Beryl had been introduced to Hannah's fist.

Hannah's voice was never quiet at the best of times and, through years of calling cattle together with the aid of powerful lungs, it had developed a strength and volume that was quite intimidating. Both Brian and Beryl Harris were short – he with wispy hair, thin as a rake, with no chin; she, the size of a small cow, her made-up 'china doll' face almost buried in the rolls of fat that surrounded it.

They found, to their bewildered surprise, this farmer's wife far different from what they had imagined her to be.

When Inspector Peters and Constable Manders arrived at the scene, they saw that a small crowd had collected, which included the Seymour boy on his bike and the three American soldiers arriving for the milking. Hannah was holding the Harris couple at bay with a heavy yard broom, which had long dangerous bristles.

Peters sighed, and getting out of the car, moved towards the group. Manders, tall and powerful looking, strode forward firmly, ready for anything.

"I thought I was through with all this when I left Kings Cross and came to this little village," Peters muttered, then raised his voice. "First of all, I take it that these soldiers are here to work, so men would you go on down to the milking shed. Miss Flinders, would you go with them and get the work started; I imagine that Dan is down there already," he looked enquiringly at the girl, who nodded. "Righto then, off you go." Sally and the soldiers quickly left.

Peters turned to Alexander. He pointed his finger at the boy. "You! Get on your bike and get on home; there is nothing here for you; if I see you still hanging around here in two minutes I'll deal with you." He advanced a couple of steps towards Alex, who jumped on his bike and pedalled quickly away.

Peters manoeuvred himself until he was standing on the steps of the house with both Mrs Kelly and the Harris couple, standing before him. "Now, Mrs Kelly, you are an honest and truthful woman.

Tell me exactly what has happened here."

"Honest ..." spluttered Beryl Harris, indignantly. Peters turned on her.

"Be quiet, or I'll run you in for disturbing the peace." Beryl gaped at the policeman. "Yes, Mrs Kelly?"

"Inspector, these people came here, demanded to be put up in the house, accused Dan of murdering their daughter, then told me to get them a cup of tea as they were tired after their travelling." Hannah was still stunned by the rudeness of the people.

Peters, with Manders standing beside him, looked down at the parents of the dead girl. "Mr and Mrs Harris, in other normal cir-cumstances, I would be offering my heart-felt condolences to you on the death of your daughter. However, I'm surprised to see you here today; I was told that you would not be free until Sunday, when the races were over."

"It's a bloody lie," Beryl Harris shouted, taking from her purse a tiny pink handkerchief and dabbing her eyes. "I'll sue who ever said that; it has broken our hearts, this death has. But, come on, who said that about us?"

"Well, actually it was the Newcastle police; they know both of you well," Peters answered calmly. "But that's beside the point. You are here and you'll be glad to know that you can now claim the body, it has been released. You are free to go ahead with your plans for the funeral. I imagine you'll be anxious to arrange that."

"Just a minute, just a minute," broke in the husband. "What about Jean's things? She must have money owing her, from this woman here, or has she taken any money she found in her room?" Manders, on his own initiative, quietly took hold of Hannah's arm, and gently removed the broom from her hands; it could prove a dangerous weapon.

"Why, you ..." began Hannah. Peters immediately interrupted.

"Mr Harris, I would advise you to be very careful in what you say. You have already, it is alleged, accused Mr Dan Kelly of the murder; now you are accusing Mrs Kelly of theft. Let me tell you I was present, when the room was searched and we found over one thousand pounds of money, hidden in her drawer ..."

"One thousand pounds!" gasped Mr Harris, his eyes gleaming at the amount. "Well, we'll take possession of that for a start, won't we Beryl?"

"Too bloody right we will."

"I'm sorry to blight your hopes, but the money has been confiscated by the police; it is the result of complicity in a black market gang in which your daughter was a leading figure. That's where the money came from." The couple from Newcastle were furious.

"And she kept it all to herself; she could have cut us in on it, the tricky bitch!" Hannah flinched at the mother's words.

"Good God, how could you say such a thing; the girl was your daughter!" Hannah cried.

"Daughter!" screeched the mother. "She was a worthless slut! Never did a thing for us; ran after every pair of trousers that offered her money; left us as soon as she could get away and also left us with bills of hers that we had to pay, what's more."

Mr Harris continued in the same vein. "And, put us to all the expense of this long journey. Well, she can damn well stay here. I'm not paying for any funeral for her; she did nothing for us. Just when she could have been letting us in on whatever game she was into, she gets killed. A waster she was, a real waster, unreliable – you could never count on her."

Hannah could stand no more. "Get out of my yard. Go back to your precious Newcastle. The bus will be here in about five minutes. I'll send Jean's possessions on to you. Don't worry about the funeral; I'll see that the poor lass – silly girl that she was – has a Christian burial. You two creatures besmirch the name of parents. Go on, get out and take your cases with you; you'll not be stepping into my house."

Hannah moved away from Manders' restraining arm and moved

towards the visitors, who hastily left the yard and actually ran out the gate to the bus stop, on the other side of the road.

To everyone's relief the bus was early and soon appeared. The driver was surprised to see his passengers going back again to the station, with all their luggage. He actually whistled when he saw the woman's eye. Jim Fellows looked across at the Kelly house, waved to the inspector and winked at Mrs Kelly, as he calmly demanded the fare from his irate, disgruntled passengers.

There was dead silence for a few minutes back at the house. Hannah was starting to feel foolish; in her embarrassment, she could only think of offering the men a cup of tea. They thanked her, but declined. Peters only wanted to check on one thing and then they could leave.

"Mrs Kelly. Did you really mean it when you said you would pay for the funeral?"

"Oh course, I meant it," snapped Hannah. "What sort of parents would treat their own flesh and blood like that? I'll see Mr Norman, he won't charge anything and I'll get Annie to help me. She would feel exactly the same as I do about the matter. It's not a matter of liking the girl; it's a matter of doing what's right."

Peters thanked the woman again and said he would inform the relevant authorities, otherwise the body would become what was called a 'Police Removal'. It would then be buried, without ceremony, in a pauper's grave. The two men shook hands gravely with Hannah and left the farm.

As they climbed wearily into the car, Peters said: "Now, there's only our meeting back at the pub. Thank God, the day's nearly over."

SIXTY-FIVE

Telephone call from the city to Bexford North at five o'clock Saturday afternoon.

"You know who this is, so listen carefully; I have a lot to tell you."

"Right, go ahead … *WHAT*? You're kidding! How on earth can we do that?"

"I'm telling you, that's the new order I received; you have to pass it on to him."

"But *how* can I tell him to do that? There's already a murder enquiry going on here."

"We know all about that; it's not important. What is important is that you do as you're told; you know the rules."

"Did you realise that the police have the girl's money? That's definite now. Seems she'd hidden it in her room."

"Oh course, we know that. She was swindling us, the rotten tart. She robbed us blind. And remember, you recommended her! The boss has not forgotten that."

"How the hell was I to know she'd do that? She bloody well did every other thing I told her she must do, even the things she hated."

"I'm not interested in excuses. For the first job, it's vital that we try to block off all clues to the activities *now*. Even if Liveridge talks his head off at the police station, if there's no definite *physical evidence*, it's still only suspicion, nothing more. But this new job is urgent; time is short. One thing in your favour; the boss was pleased with you getting Liveridge to use the truck, to shift the merchandise last night. The boss said, now that the goods are out of sight and well hidden, there's only this one more job you have to do."

"But *how* the hell am I going to do that? It's impossible! He'll refuse."

"He hasn't in the past; he's done everything you asked of him."

"But I can't see *how* he can do it. It's physically impossible!"

"Shut up, I'm tired of your nervous vapours; we've had news from an informer; we've got it all carefully worked out – it just requires split second timing, that's all … Now listen carefully …"

SISTY-SIX

Annie Watson, before she had summonsed up courage to tell her husband of her offer to take the Darcy children, was delighted when Constable Watkins forestalled her, by ringing to say the father had been released and was back home.

The constable had thanked her sincerely for her generous offer. It was with a relieved mind, that Annie was able to talk with Sam about the visit of their daughter and her husband tomorrow morning, as they sat near the fire, before she started preparations for an early evening meal.

"And Sam, remember, they will be coming with us – as well as Susan and Reg Cerney with their kids – to Mass at Wembley Hospital chapel, so it'll be a very, very crowded car – I don't know if we'll fit them all in – but we'll manage, won't we? They'll have to sit on laps; that's the only way." Annie closed her eyes counting in her mind the number of passengers.

"Sam, if we put four in the back – that's Penny and George, Reg and Sue with the baby – Reg can hold young Ben on his lap – then, in the front we could have Norah as well as you and me. Pretty crowded, Sam."

"Could be a good thing, love; the more, the better, I think, considering everything."

"You're right. I want to take Norah to help with the kids, but I didn't think we could fit her in." Annie smiled fondly. "Isn't it funny,

Sam, Norah putting her hair up, now she's in charge of the infants? She insists they call her 'Aunty', and to everyone's surprise, is doing a wonderful job. She's like one of those fairy book characters – everyone's Nanny.

"I bet she'll be exactly the same when she is sixty or seventy, sweet and innocent, yet very strict and everyone will adore her as they do now." Annie reached across and placed her hand gently on her husband's arm. "You know, Sam, we've been very blessed, haven't we? Not only in our own children, but in the friends we have here. I know I have been, in finding you."

"I haven't done too badly myself, dear. Mind you, you've given me most of my grey hairs, but as the Irish say: you're a loving woman, Annie Watson. Now, dear, just belt up will you and keep quiet; I want to hear the early evening news, with the day's war reports. I think, after dinner, we should make it an early night. We've got a big day ahead of us tomorrow."

SIXTY-SEVEN

The suspects had been sent home and the police meeting was in progress at the pub. The lights were on, and the blackout blinds in place.

"Right, Pierce, tell us the suspects you think of as definite candidates for the murder." Peters stretched out his legs and leaned back in his chair. The policemen were sitting casually around the table, all equally weary, hoping the meeting would not continue for very much longer.

Sergeant Pierce consulted his pad reading from his notes. "Well, I think we most definitely have Alan Darcy, Gerald Seymour and Toby Moore. They were at the pub, they each spoke separately to Jean; they each left the pub after she had left – and all claim they chatted outside for up to an hour, before they went home – that's a long time for a chat. None of them has a real alibi as they all alibi each other."

Peters scribbled on his pad. "So, three definite suspects, as regards time and opportunity. I wonder if we have another one."

"Sir?"

"Well, I'm having difficulty with this one, chaps, but I've got a sneaking feeling that the murder is not straight forward, or 'gang-related' at all. I'm beginning to think it's more likely to be what Annie Watson suggested, a passionate murder."

"Sir?" Both Manders and Watkins spoke together, their faces

puzzled. Constable Potts came to their assistance.

"Inspector, I don't think the youngsters understand what you're saying. I do, unfortunately and I can see where this is heading," Potts said, his brow furrowed. "That's a horrible thought."

"Trust you, Potsy," Peters smiled. "Well, lads, I meant that I think the murder was committed by someone who actually *did* love the wretched girl; or did love her at one time …"

"And was ditched by her!" finished Potts.

"Constable Potts is right. And that leads me straight to the young ones. I, personally, have to be very careful here. I'm aware that I am stupidly prejudiced about Otto's origins, which, I know, is ridiculous. Everyone in this room, including myself, is at least *part* German, through our English heritage.

"However, think about this: a young man, his first experience with a girl; he falls madly in love with her; she grants him favours he has only dreamed about – then she dumps him. It's a familiar theme and, unfortunately, the result is one that we see all too often.

"And it's not just Otto I'm thinking of. I'm worried about another one: Ron Perry. I'm worried, I think I've been too easy with him because of his good wife. However, let's look at him seriously. He's a young man, good looking, infatuated with the beautiful young woman. He wouldn't be the first young married man to be bowled over by a siren. We only have his word that he was going to end it all, don't we? Perhaps she ditched him, not the other way around. Let's keep Perry in the frame."

Peters turned again to his Sergeant. "Pierce, what do you think?"

"Sir, I accept what you are suggesting and it's true we've seen this before, but I can't get away from the facts you found in the book you discovered. To me, it's the key to the murderer. I am sure Gerald Seymour is the obvious leader of the gang, for this area; he received the most money and has most to lose from those mysterious bosses, BW and AL, if it were found out that Jean was robbing the till. They would easily think he was in collusion with her."

Peters nodded his head at Pierce's reasoning, then suddenly yawned. He was dead tired and decided to call it a day. "Come on, chaps, we've had enough for today but, before we go, I want each of you young chaps to tell me who you think the murderer could be … Sergeant Pierce says Seymour, what about you Watkins?"

Watkins flushed. "I really have no idea, sir, but I think the same way as Sergeant Pierce does. It's the money that convinces me every time; it's a small fortune Seymour received."

"Manders?"

"Well, I certainly do understand your thinking regarding the possibilities of being ditched by Jean as you just now mentioned in regard to Ron Perry. That's something that a man, young or old, doesn't take lightly. I was thinking of the first girl I fell for; I was deliriously happy – I thought I had found the girl of my dreams. I was only fourteen years old at the time, but when she dumped me and went with an older boy at school, I was actually alternating between writing suicide notes – and murder plots."

The young Constable started to laugh. "Now you know, sir, the sort of policeman you have on your staff – a possible murderer – at least in theory anyway."

Everyone laughed. Peters eyed his protégé closely.

"Well, there's an honest man! I think each and every one of us could kill, if we felt that our most precious loved one was in danger, so we're all possible murderers, and never are we so emotionally unstable, as when we're adolescents; our hormones are going crazy." The Inspector stood up. "Well, having said that, let's go home. Nothing's likely to happen tonight."

With the benefit of hindsight, as it turned out, that was one of the greatest miscalculations Peters had ever made.

SIXTY-EIGHT

Alexander climbed out his bedroom window when it was good and dark. The wind had dropped, so although it was cold, it was not freezing, as it had been the night before.

However, he took with him a thick sweater, with his favourite scarf, as well as his blanket. There was no need to worry about being seen as there was only a little slip of a moon, so with the blackout, it was black as pitch, as usual, outside.

Alex hurried across the road to his hiding spot behind the bins near the trough, but first he made sure he placed the tin for the money in its rightful place underneath. He was excited; tonight should be much better than last night; everyone has had time to find their letter by now. Alex mused on the amount he would receive in the tin. He'd see how much it was tonight; he'd then leave it for a week, or, perhaps ten days, then he'd send more letters, raising the price.

Really, he smiled gleefully, there's no end to possibilities here – it could be a gold mine. The future looked brighter than it had ever been since they came to live in this dump. Alex thought that, in time, he could even get to like this place after all.

Some hours later, Alex thought he was dreaming as he was dragged to his feet by the back of his collar, but he came awake rapidly as someone slapped him viciously back and forth, across the face. He whimpered in terror, as the hand moved to his chest and was holding him helpless, a little off the ground. He went to scream as he felt something gouge into his back, but only a gurgling sound came forth, from the open mouth; his mind was screaming inside his head with the pain … the searing, agonizing, paralysing pain … he never knew such pain was possible … his lips were stretched back in agony …

In his death throes, impaled as he was, his body twisting into grotesque shapes, twitching uncontrollably; Alex for a short period, unknowingly, actually imitated the cat, Mingy … in *its* death agony … His eyes fluttered briefly opened… then glazed in agony…

…He died slowly and horribly.

SIXTY-NINE

Major Tim Johnson was not a churchgoer, but on Sundays, he liked to take a good long walk to get out of the pub – and the smell of beer – for an hour.

He usually went by the Old Lane, at the back of the Watson place, but this Sunday, for no reason, he decided to stick to the main road. The air was sharply cold, but there was no biting wind. There was frost in the air and Tim breathed in deeply the beautiful, clean fresh air.

Tim smiled as he passed the shops, thinking about the new owners of the General Store. They were pleasant people; how difficult for them, having a German name. Past the shops, he looked in admiration at the Watson house with lights already showing through the edges of the blackout blinds; they were obviously getting ready for Church.

He walked on only a few steps, at a brisk pace, when he suddenly halted. Out of the corner of his eye he saw someone, or something, moving near the old Feed and Grain store – opposite the Seymour house. Surely not a burglar, at this hour of the morning! No, it's not some*one* but some*thing*, hanging there … something …near the loading dock.

Tim moved closer, then staggered and nearly fell, his eyes goggling in disbelief at what he saw. He gagged at the horror, the vomit rising in his throat. He tried to shout, but no sound would come. He felt his legs giving way.

Tim closed his eyes and forced himself to be still. He swallowed the bile in his throat in a noisy gulp and then opening his eyes, stared at Alexander hanging above him … on one of the loading hooks from the store … the sharp hook had gone right through the boy's back … ripping open his front. Gore and bloody intestines had poured out in profusion, while, with the face a grotesque mask of terror, the mouth open in agony, it was a spectre from a nightmare!

What to do? Who to call? Automatically, without conscious awareness of doing so, Tim ran down the Watson's path to the front door and hammered on it, calling frantically. The door was opened suddenly by Sam wearing his pyjamas.

"What the hell …?"

"Sam, ring the police … another murder … the Seymour kid … I think … I thinnnn …" Tim gave a gentle sigh and fainted. He would have fallen had not Sam grabbed him in time. Sam called loudly for his wife.

"Annie, come quickly for the love of God! Another bloody one murdered. Hurry up … you've got to take Tim, I'll call the police."

SEVENTY

Annie Watson having scrambled into her Sunday clothes, after dealing with Tim – who was now lying on a sofa in their lounge room – was trying to think of a number of things at the one time. With tremendous difficulty, she marshalled her thoughts.

First of all, Tim: she must deal with him. She rang the pub and explained to a startled Betty, that her husband was recovering from shock in their house. Betty, horrified, promised to get the car out and come and get him. Annie informed Betty of the murder, but aware of her condition, urged her not to even look in the Feed and Grain store, for her own safety – she then called to her husband.

"Sam, get dressed as quickly as you can. I want you to get the car out, drive to the McKenzies, wait there until it's time for us to go to Church, then let George and Penny get into the back seat of the car from McKenzie's place, rather than from here.

"I'll have the rest of the crowd ready for you when you get here; don't come right up to our house, Sam; I'll have the crowd waiting directly opposite the Seymour house near the shops – that'll save them from standing waiting where they could see Alex hanging; from what you've said, we'd be out of the way of the police as well.

"But, hurry dear, the police will be here soon and I'll have to see them and…" she suddenly shouted, as she remembered: "Good God! There's the boy's mother, Elise. I'd completely forgotten her! But first things first, I must ring Harriet."

Annie rushed to the phone, informed Harriet and George of the new tragedy and of the changed plans for the collection of the two young people. "I think, Harriet, that'll be easier with all the people who will be milling around here when the police arrive and the word spreads … Sorry, I have to go, dear, the police will arrive any minute, and I must see the poor mother."

Annie called out as she left the house. "That clear, love?" She heard a grunt and ran across to the Seymour's cottage. She paused, momentarily, looked at the hideous sight of the child hanging, shut her eyes in horror, crossing herself, quickly.

Her urgent knocking on the door resulted finally in it being opened by Elise, clutching her dressing gown tightly around her night clothes. She looked bewildered at her visitor at this time of the morning. This was made worse by Annie taking the woman into her arms and holding her tightly.

"I'm so sorry, Elise, I know how you must feel, for if anything happened to my own boy, I think I'd die …" Elise Seymour managed to untangle herself a little.

"Mrs Watson, I mean … Annie … is something the matter?"

"Oh, idiot that I am, I thought you already knew. Yes, something dreadful has happened. Is your husband up yet?"

"Yes, he rises early; he's out in the back garden I think. Anyhow, he was not in the bed when I heard you knock. But what's happened."

Annie took a deep breath. "It's Alex, Elise …" Annie got no chance to say another word. Elise screamed, a thin, piercing sound. "What do you mean, it's Alex? What has happened to him? Where is he? No … don't hold me Annie. I want to see him."

Pushing past Annie, Elise stumbled out the door and looking left, then right, saw her son lit suddenly by the rays of the morning sun: saw him hanging in all the grotesque horrors of his gargoyle condition, as though highlighted by spotlights.

All thoughts of her attire gone, Elise flew barefoot through the gate and across the Lane shrieking hysterically, in her shock. She ran straight into the arms of Inspector Peters, as he stepped out of his car.

Peters grabbed the woman, holding her tightly with both arms. "Pierce, ring through for an ambulance, the police surgeon and for Dr Kemp. Tell them I want them all immediately. Then get on to Manders, Watkins and Potts again; tell them to hurry up; they must get here, as quickly as they can." The inspector spotted Nan Brady hurrying towards the scene. "Mrs Brady, would you help Mrs Watson with this woman, until Dr Kemp gets here; she'll need sedating. This is a frightful sight."

Nan Brady hurried to Annie who indicated the monstrosity hanging about them.

Nan blanched and trembled, taking two steps backwards, muttering a startled oath. She whispered to Annie, "Not that I ever liked the poor kid – I thought he was horrible, but this is how they butcher pigs, not human beings. The murderer must be insane, a monster!"

"You've said it, Nan," Annie spoke quietly, deliberately keeping her eyes away from the sight of what was hanging above them. She moved forward and with her old friend's help, managed to get Elise Seymour out of Peters' arms and led her gently back to her own home.

Elise had quietened a little, but kept darting looks back over her shoulder, and shuddering violently each time she did so; her thin shoulders hunched and with hysteria only a panting breath away.

"Where's the damn husband I'd like to know," Annie murmured over Elise's head, "anyhow, Nan, we'll take the poor woman into her own front room and get a blanket to keep her warm. I'll try to rouse up the daughter, to make her mother a cup of strong tea with plenty of sugar."

"I'll do that, Annie," Nan said. "Peters said he wanted to speak to you. You go, and when Dr Kemp arrives, just send him to me here. I'll stay with her."

SEVENTY-ONE

When Sam Watson drove back with his two special passengers, to pick up his wife and their neighbours – the Cerneys with their children and Norah – he thought Annie's foresight in suggesting the car wait down from their own place and directly opposite Seymour's, had been a sound idea.

It would have been impossible to be able to park in front of their own house with the clutter of vehicles that were now, either in Sheridan Lane, or in the main road. A surprisingly large crowd of onlookers had gathered there as well when the news of the murder had spread.

Sam saw that Norah was already there waiting to help the children settle in the car. He hoped she hadn't seen the murdered boy, or if she had, that she hadn't understood it.

Dr Kemp had been with Elise Seymour, she was now in the care of his wife, Thelma, a trained nursing sister. Kemp stood near the dead boy waiting for the Police Surgeon; they would work together, getting the child down from the hook.

Sam was pleased to see that Annie had, indeed, marshalled their carload and were, ready for collection at the chosen spot – away from the abomination hanging near the water-trough.

SEVENTY-TWO

The gunman watched through the window gritting his teeth at the number of people. He forced himself to relax, resting his rifle comfortably on the window sill. His target was invisible at the moment, but if his guess was correct, the target would make a mistake any minute now, and that would be the only chance there was.

He must make sure he didn't miss: everything now depended on this, one, single, shot. He had been nervous with apprehension, when he was first told what he had to do, now he was surprised to realise he was utterly calm.

SEVENTY-THREE

Annie had spoken to Inspector Peters and told him all she knew. Tim Johnson had been collected by his wife; Annie also informed Peters of the important extra passengers they were carrying to Mass that morning who were already in the car.

Peters nodded his approval of the plan as Annie walked back to their car.

In the back seat of the car, George McKenzie and his wife Penny sat holding hands tightly. Then one of those little accidents occurred, which threw all the security arrangements awry.

Reg Cerney, carrying his small son, was waiting while his wife, Susan, holding the baby, was just about to get into the back seat, when she almost tripped on the baby's long shawl.

She had lifted her foot to step onto the running board … and stumbled. She would have fallen, had not George, forgetting all the warnings he had received, leaped from the car and grabbed Susan's arm to help her into the back seat.

For that one moment his back was totally exposed. A sharp, flat cracking sound rang out, its echoes ringing in the clear, cold air.

Young George straightened, looked at his wife, his eyes wide with surprise, and, falling backwards, dropped to the ground, striking his head on the running board, as he did so.

George McKenzie, the young Prosecutor in the trial of Al Fordham was dead!

SEVENTY-FOUR

In the few seconds after the shooting, an uncanny silence reigned in the area jammed with vehicles and people, as shock numbed the senses of the crowd.

Then Annie screamed piercingly, her voice shattering the silence in the clear, still air. Susan, grasping her baby in her arms, was staring down at the young man at her feet bewildered, then looking at Annie, in stunned disbelief.

The young Mr McKenzie couldn't possibly … be dead?

Penny had pushed past Susan, getting out of the car and now knelt on the roadway taking up the dead man in her arms. She was too shocked to even scream. With her eyes unfocused in shock, Penny simply rocked her husband of five months, back and forth, back and forth, in her arms like a baby, uttering a low wailing, inhuman, keening sound that went on and on.

Sam was clasping Annie tightly as she struggled with hysteria and then both knelt by the side, of their daughter. Nan Brady left Elise to Thelma Kemp's care and stumbling, ran over to her favourite young man, whom she had known since he was born, her eyes streaming with tears with her wails of despair echoing as they grew louder and louder.

This was horror building on horror.

The elderly woman crouched near the devastated parents of the young girl, now a widow, crying helplessly. Norah, white faced, stared in shocked bewilderment at the man lying on the road.

Annie was the first to recognize the danger to the other passengers. With her voice uneven and broken, she spoke to her blacksmith neighbour. "Reg, you can drive. Look, take the car, your family and *Norah too*; go on to Mass. This is dangerous for them to see this… as well as the other … *thing …*"

Annie looked, tearfully, at her husband, "Best, isn't it?" Sam nodded. "Right, Reg, off you go. Quickly now, this is no place for them – it's a place of horrors. *Reg …REG! Look at me! Remember you have NORAH with you.*"

Reg, in shock, looked at poor Norah; she was staring, her eyes enormous; her mouth open, at the first dead person she had ever seen. Reg, then, nodded his understanding, hurriedly packing Norah and everyone into the car.

As it quickly left the scene, Annie slumped down on the road, her tears falling freely, her strength now utterly gone.

* * *

For Annie time and sound were no longer real. She felt as though she had entered a nightmare state – a new dimension; the scene kept shifting in and out of focus; sounds came, went: now loud, now whisper quiet. In a dream-like manner she was dimly aware of Inspector Peters shouting incomprehensible orders to his men somewhere a long way off and she became fixated on a little bird high up on the telegraph wires. She vaguely wondered what it was doing here; was it related to one of the dead, or was it a soul escaping the confines of a body?

To Annie it was all unreal even the little bird; she wondered if she had died, or was trapped in a violent nightmare from which she couldn't wake; she was vaguely surprised to find Harriet and George – both distraught – kneeling beside Penny on the road. To Annie it seemed they had materialized from nowhere; she puzzled as to where they had come from and, for a moment, wondered *who* they were.

The McKenzies were numb with shock as they saw their only child dead in the arms of his wife. Annie watched, stricken, as the parents' hands kept reaching out to touch George, as if to see whether it was real or not – if, *it had really happened!*

Annie wanted to scream and scream: *This was your child!* It isn't a nightmare! But no sound came out.

Annie saw the others through the medium of her own delirium; she wondered vaguely if she could wake up, or whether she even *wanted* to wake up. Not even the sudden violent noisy avalanche of weeping erupting from Penny, as she moved from shocked disbelief, to reality, failed to arouse Annie from this deadly inability to respond to anything - everything had acquired a trance-like quality.

All she could do was to stare at the dead face of her daughter's husband, her own face white with shock, her eyes enormous.

Gradually …very, very, slowly, she became vaguely aware of Dr Kemp running across to them; it was only when he shouted loudly and very sharply to Annie, that his voice penetrated her numbness; it was only then she felt the pain of the hard gravel under her knees.

"Annie, Annie, look at me!" Kemp kept shouting, suddenly afraid for her. She looked vaguely puzzled at the man calling her name. What on earth did he want? Why won't he just go away? She tried to lift her eyes to his, but it was too exhausting.

She made an effort to speak, to concentrate. *Who* was it? Oh, yes, the doctor. What was his name …was it, Edward? …Oh *yes*, Edward... She *knew* Edward.

"Edward? Edward, Young George has been shot; he's been shot …Penny's George is dead, Edward; George is dead … He's just a boy, Edward – he's dead!"

Dr Edward Kemp slowly lifted Annie to her feet and just as slowly he spoke slowly and authoritatively. "Yes, Annie, George is dead. But I want *you* to stand up now, and look at the wound with me, will you? I *need* you to pay attention now …you're good at this … you know you are …*you-can-help-me.* You can help me to find the wicked person who killed *George*."

Still holding on to Annie tightly, Kemp spoke loudly to Sam. "Sam, would you turn the body on its side, facing you for a moment. I just need to see the entry wound; we can see the exit one."

Sam, kneeling by Penny's side, took the body from her arms and placing one hand on the shoulder and the other on back of the thigh, turned the body towards himself. Kemp felt Annie withdraw herself from his hold. The terrible sight of the bloody wound pierced through Annie's mental inertia.

"Edward, it's wrong," she muttered, her eyes widening and clearing, fixed on the gaping wound. She raised her voice: "Edward …*it's WRONG!*"

"What is?" Kemp was mystified. He had only asked Annie to look in order to bring her back to reality.

Annie paused, still staring at the wound while her mind replayed in slow motion the scene of the death. George had jumped out of the car to help Susan and, in doing so, his back was exposed to the street as he *stood by the side of* the car with his back to the engine – to the *FRONT of the car, not facing the Seymour house or the shops opposite*!

He had been reaching for Susan's arm – to steady her – when the shot had struck him; the heavy gauge bullet crashing through the back to the heart.

Annie, trance-like, pointed to the *entry* wound.

"It's a straight line," she mumbled, as though mesmerised, "from back to front!"

"Yes, my dear, a bullet always fires straight, just like that, from back to front." Kemp's voice softened, soothingly, "Annie, as you said, it's a straight line and it's in a straight line with Seymour's house; Peters knows where the gun shot came from – and who the murderer is."

She slowly raised her eyes from the body and looked at the buildings opposite. Then, keeping her arm straight, Annie moved her hand from the entry wound and slowly turned, keeping the arm rigidly stiff so it was in a perfect straight line with the wound.

She paused as she saw where the fingers of her hand were pointing; the *direction* from which the shot *must* have come.

"Edward," she called urgently, "the *angle*! The *entry* wound is in an oblique, straight line to the *exit* wound. It points to where the shot came from."

At that moment Annie, trembling violently, realised who had killed Young George; in fact, who had done all the murders. "*Oh! Please God, no!*" she cried loudly.

Her brain tuned into the general, noisy clamour of the police and she became aware of Inspector Peters.

The Inspector, for the first time in his career in the Force, had been so shocked by the horrific death of the child, then actually witnessing a murder before his eyes, had lost control – his brain was spinning; it seemed to be jerking from one horror to the other. He was shouting incomprehensively in his near delirium. Sergeant Pierce, with quick understanding, rushed to Peters' side and taking a firm hold of his arm, spoke sharply to his boss: "Now, just stay quiet sir, it's all right – it's only me, Pierce, sir; come on sir, we *need* you – I'll do the work, but you must stay with me; just leave it to us, we'll fix it ; just rest a bit with me; it's a terrible shock – the worst I've seen … just rest easy, sir…close your eyes…that's right…just a few deep breaths…good, now lean on me, sir… just lean on me."

Peters shook his head, coming back from the edge, turned his head and saw his Sergeant's pale, troubled face. "Sorry, Pierce, ashamed …but such agony… such suffering… anguish…"

Holding tightly onto the Inspector, Pierce rapidly took over the situation determined that as few people as possible would observe Peters' condition. He gave orders to the Constables firmly and authoritatively, in a loud voice:

"Bring out Seymour! He may, or may not, have been involved in the killing of Jean and then his own son – if he did, he's a monster – but he *definitely killed this good young man* –in a dead straight line from his house. He *has* to be in the pay of Al Fordham to have done that,"

At the mention of the gangster's name, Pierce was interrupted by Peters who shouted loudly, coming out of his mental fog. "Al Fordham, AF! God in Heaven, Pierce! How could I have been so stupid! Fordham's been behind everything here – the murders and the whole black market! He must have ordered the killing of Young George; otherwise nothing makes sense."

Then, with a return to his usual form, Peters ordered: "Yes, the Sergeant's right; do as he told you: Bring out Seymour; he killed the young man. And," he looked across the road at the tableau on the ground, "Mrs Watson is right, too, I'm sure of that now. Jean's death was nothing to do with the gang; it was a passionate killing, so bring out OE ... Otto Eckhard – *I'm going to charge him with Jean's death.* It *WAS a passionate murder*; no pussy-footing around, gloves off now; we're dealing with murderers."

As the constables hesitated, embarrassed and bewildered, knowing that something was wrong, Peters shouted angrily at his men: "What are you waiting for? Get the two murdering bastards *NOW* and drag them here!"

Annie was dimly aware, in all the shouting and commotion that Inspector Peters soon had the two men handcuffed to the railing of the trough, where they stood under the hanging entrails of Alexander. The boy, Otto, began to cry in his terror at the horrific sight; his mother in tears clinging to her husband who looked stupefied at what he was seeing.

Annie willed herself to move; she knew somehow she *must MOVE* and ... she must speak quickly, or a terrible miscarriage of justice would take place.

Inspector Peters' voice continued. "Say what you have to say,

Pierce. Read them their rights and take them away ..."

A trembling, but still clear, carrying voice interrupted him, calling urgently and loudly.

"No. No, Inspector ... I'm sorry, but they didn't kill anyone. They may be guilty of other things, *but not murder*; you have made a mistake; the angle of the wound is wrong – it's not from Seymour's place or the shops – and you have the *wrong* OE ..."

"*WHAT*?" Peters shouted loudly, turning in his surprise to Annie, who was coming towards him from across the road, her walk unsteady as if she were sleep-walking, her eyes not on Peters, seemingly unfocused.

Annie moved through the crowd of people, not even aware of them and stood near the water-trough. She looked past the Inspector and spoke to the shadowy corner of the Store where the bins were standing.

"Come out Eric. I know you're there behind the bins. It's all over now ... as soon as I heard the initials OE I knew it stood for Old Eric. It does, doesn't it? ... They even made a fool of you by calling you that – those vile, evil people ... Come on, Eric, it's only Miss Anne here ... What would my mother, the Lady Mary, whom you loved, think of this, eh? She respected you highly.

"Put down the rifle, Eric ... you didn't want to kill anyone, I know that ... Come on Eric ... please Eric, please, for Lady Mary's sake ... You don't want to see a young boy, who is innocent, punished for these terrible crimes, do you? ... If you came out now, and told the truth, Eric, Lady Mary would then be so proud of you ... if you would do just that ... *Please, please* Eric, I beg you ..."

There was complete silence. Every one present held their breath wondering if Annie had gone mad. Sam began to walk, uncertainly, towards his wife. As they waited, in a terror-filled silence, an old man, bent, gaunt, wrinkled, pathetic in his helplessness, walked slowly forward, the rifle dangling loosely in his hand, the barrel pointing to the road. Annie, crying openly, looked sadly at the murderer. The old man fixed his eyes on Annie.

"Oh, Eric," Annie cried, her voice breaking with emotion, "how could you do such a dreadful, dreadful thing?"

The old man dropped the rifle, his eyes filled with tears; he knelt on the ground and cried like a child.

Annie turned to the police, her face tragic. "He's all yours, Inspector. Treat him gently, I beg of you – the poor, poor dear old man."

SEVENTY-FIVE

It was Monday evening before Inspector Peters was able to call on the Watsons. It had been a hectic two days. Eric Munroe had been charged with three counts of murder and had made a full confession. He also confessed to being a member of the black market gang and gave the police the evidence they needed to convict Gerald Seymour of being the local 'Boss' for the gangster Al Fordham's organization.

Eric had also informed the police, as an important member of the Government Agricultural Allocation Committee, Seymour had syphoned off many of the allowances owing to farmers into his own account. This had been discovered by Barry Wilson, Fordham's right-hand-man and Fordham offered Seymour the chance of gaining even more money through taking charge of one of the branches of his enterprises.

It was Seymour who first discovered the girl Jean Harris to be a useful tool, using her to recruit other men in the village through her overt seductive talent. Bert Liveridge and Alan Darcy had been the most heavily involved, with Toby Moore slightly less; however, they would all receive long prison sentences, Inspector Peters, assured Annie and Sam.

Others on the list who had not received payment for their involvement would receive more lenient treatment; this included Ron Perry who would most probably only get a fine, if anything. But Bert Liveridge, with all the obvious signs of his involvement for everyone to see – his truck and his entire new front room furniture – was, sadly, in Peters' opinion – in for a rough time. He would not only receive the longest sentence in goal, but would have all the goods impounded; how poor Lily Liveridge would cope with that, was anyone's guess.

"Now that Darcy will undoubtedly go to gaol, Mrs Watson, it means that Mrs Darcy will have to continue work to support the family. I was hoping she would be kept away from the Hospital with all those men there," Peters sighed, "but Policewoman Adams assures me she will keep a vigilant eye on what goes on in that household."

Annie listened to the policeman, while in her mind she was wondering if she could get Rosemary a job as a trainee nursery maid for Mrs Perry – that might work.

Peters cleared his throat. "Mr and Mrs Watson, I don't know how to say this but I feel responsible for Young George McKenzie's death, even for the boy Alexander." Both Annie and Sam looked at Peters in surprise.

"But why is that, Inspector?" queried Sam. "I think the police did everything they could think of all these past weeks, trying to protect George. Surely it had nothing to do with you; it was another department who directed the security arrangements."

"Nevertheless, I feel responsible. I knew about Gerald Seymour and intended to take him in Saturday, but it was such a rotten day and we were so exhausted at the end of it, I foolishly said, we'd leave it as nothing would happen that night – in fact *everything* happened that night: the boy was murdered – gruesomely – and then Young George was executed right in front of our eyes the next morning.

"I'm sure you witnessed my disgrace at the scene of the crime. That had never happened to me before; I think it was the combination of all the horrors happening at once. I don't honestly know what would have happened had not my very loyal friend, Sergeant Pierce, rescued me. I owe him a debt I can never repay. He is not only an excellent officer, but he's a fine and a truly good man. They're rare to find. It was he who realised something else that should have twigged with me.

"Sergeant Pierce kept saying that there was something wrong with the blackmail letters. I knew there was, but couldn't see what it was. Really incredible blindness!

"The writing was too perfect: each letter, each capital, beautifully executed in a perfect copperplate style; that is not the style of blackmail letters – it is the style of a school child, trying his best to write perfectly; to write as he think adults do. So, as a group, let me say we do not feel very proud of ourselves."

The Inspector smiled ruefully. "I know it's always easier to know what you should have done after the event, but truly, I shouldn't have expected that everyone would just wait, until we were rested."

Annie sat up straight, her voice suddenly severe. She spoke sharply. "Inspector, just stop it this minute. If anyone is to blame, I am. I knew Eric was infatuated with Jean Harris, Charlie told me.

"I tried several time to hint that you should look at the old ones, but I couldn't bring myself to actually mention Eric as the OE you were looking for. I've known him all my life, and remember sitting on their counter as a little girl, with Eric giving me sweets.

"I know perfectly well that's no excuse at all, but I truly did not dream that he would do what he actually did. But I should have! To be ditched at his age! You don't just shrug that off!

"But there is no blame on your part, or the part of any of the police. You, personally, have been worked like a slave ever since this rotten war began and you're still at it – you can never call a single day your own; you carry immense responsibility for a huge area and you are not God. You are a human being who was simply exhausted; you are not omniscient." Annie smiled gently. "No, I didn't notice the little 'incident', my dear Inspector, but I did hear about it. But, what about me; I was like a mad woman. Wandering all over the road…"

Her voice softened. "There has not been one hint of blame

attached to either you, or the other department, from Harriet and George, or even from Penelope. They think all the effort the police made to try to protect George since the Trial began, has been magnificent. Penny – whom we have been with all day at the Hospital – asked me to personally thank you; she said how lucky she was to have you there, when it all happened."

"Mrs Watson, I was afraid to ask before. Did they manage to save the baby?" Peters saw the tears starting in Annie's eyes. "I see, they didn't! I am so very sorry for you, for your daughter and for those good people George and Harriet McKenzie."

"Thank you Inspector. It is heartbreaking but then, that's life isn't it? Penny is coping with it better than I thought she would. She will remain in Hospital for a little longer, then she will come home, not here, but to the McKenzies.

"I think that's right. Harriet and George have lost everything, including their future grandchild; they will never have another. We have lost a wonderful son-in-law, but we still have both our children. I'm so glad that Penny loves both her in-laws; she is happy to be going to stay with them." Annie had another problem on her conscience.

"Inspector Peters, I must apologise for shouting out in public that you had made a mistake. I truly don't know what was wrong with me – I was like a zombie walking. I suppose it was the dreadful shock. When I 'came to', all I could think of was the innocent young lad, Otto, being charged with a crime he didn't commit."

"Please, Mrs Watson," begged Peters, "don't apologise! I was nearly off my head. You saved me! Don't you realise if you hadn't interrupted me I would have made a criminal mistake; in all likelihood, I would have been unable to convict Gerald Seymour, of all his other crimes; the charges would be thrown out of court because of my error."

"Well, thank you, but I still think I did it in a rude and insensitive manner."

Annie wanted to change the subject. "Inspector, tell me about Eric. Did he give any explanation for his terrible behaviour?"

"I was just coming to that, Mrs Watson," Peters replied. "Yes, he did. In fact he left a letter for you and asked, after I had read it, if it would be permissible for me to bring it to you."

"Oh, dear, I'm almost afraid to read it; he's been part of my entire life."

"It's a sad letter, I'm afraid. Let me read it to you – some of it is heavily underlined." Peters carefully opened the letter and keeping his eyes on the text read clearly and slowly.

"My dear and honoured Miss Anne,
I can only hope, through your kindness which has been an inspiration to me all my life, that you will read this letter from a murderer. You asked me on Sunday, why I did those <u>dreadful</u> things. Looking back I think I did it all because I was <u>frightened</u>; frightened of death which is close now and frightened that all my life I had done nothing, been nowhere, had nothing at all to show for the long life I had lived.

When Jean approached me and began, as I thought, to actually take an interest in me I couldn't believe it. She was young and beautiful: I had dreamed of meeting such a woman all my life. When she said she would marry me and come away with me, I couldn't believe all my dreams had come true. Then I discovered I had been <u>fooled</u>. Gerald Seymour informed me I had to become involved in the gang's activities as he needed the storage space, I could provide – he threatened to tell Charlie and ruin my reputation if I did not do everything he wanted. Jean said she would only continue with me if I joined up with them. I was so infatuated I would have done anything to keep her. I used to sneak out at night, to open the annexe and help with the loading, or the storing, of the merchandise.

One terrible day I overheard Jean and Gerald talking and I realised they were <u>laughing</u> at me. Jean said I made her nearly vomit when she had to touch me. I nearly went mad; all my dreams of escaping from this awful prison of a store – for that's what it's been to me – and starting a new life, even at my age, were gone. Then Gerald received word from his Boss that Jean was robbing them and ordered <u>ME</u> to kill her. I did so with <u>pleasure</u>! I, who had never in my whole life killed anything, discovered it was so easy to kill and I was nearly mad with fury at her <u>deceit</u>. Then that awful child, sending his letters! Do you know he sent one to his own father? He was a depraved <u>monster</u>! He was making fun of the only thing in my whole life that had been, in the beginning, beautiful; that had meant anything to me. I found him Saturday night waiting, behind the bins, to milk more money from his poor deluded victims, so I killed him.

I didn't have any desire to kill George McKenzie – the Mckenzies are fine and noble people. However, I had no option. Gerald informed me that the Boss had ordered it; if I refused to do it, then my previous killings would be revealed to the police. You know what happened. As I held the rifle on our window sill I understood there was no way out – I would definitely be caught now. That's why I went out to the bins; I knew it would only be a matter of time before the police caught me.

In my youth I spent hours listening spellbound to dear, beloved Sir Joseph Sheridan, your father, telling exciting stories about his life and about the life of his father in the gold fields near Bathurst. <u>I wanted so much to be like him</u>, and I was nothing but an obscure, unknown <u>nothing</u>; working all my life in a dirty and dusty store. I know now that it was the only place I was fit to be. I could never have amounted to anything.

I'm so sorry, Miss Anne. Please, can you, ever, in your heart forgive me for what I've done? If <u>you</u> can, then perhaps God will have mercy on a pathetic old man. If you are able to do so, please pray for me. <u>I hope they do hang me; it's what I deserve.</u>

Eric Munroe."

"Oh, my God!" cried Annie, openly crying. "Oh, dear God! What a lot my family has to account for! The evil we have done!"

Peters said urgently: "And the *good* as well, Mrs Watson; please, please, don't forget that, Mrs Watson, the *good* as well."

SEVENTY-SIX

The following ten days were a nightmare to Annie. To help the ladies, Major Ted Waters at the Convalescent Hospital cancelled the Occupational Therapy sessions for a fortnight. The sensational murder of 'the girl in the water-trough' had brought about a storm of press activity, but the following sequence of murders, brought it to almost incoherent frenzy.

Reporters were everywhere. Poor Penelope, after she was released from Hospital, was hounded until, in desperation, she refused to leave the McKenzie house at all – even to show herself at a window.

The press had a field day with the news that a Black Market gang had been operating out of a rural, very respectable village, with this organization directly involved in the murder of a Crown Prosecutor, excitement remained at a very high level: press photographers were anxious to get any shots they could of just about anybody at all – to accompany the endless accounts in the papers.

Annie found it difficult even to try to visit her daughter in the McKenzie house, in spite of the fact that police were posted as guards for the bereaved young widow, day and night. Mother and daughter were reduced to speaking only on the phone.

The big funeral finally took place in the old Anglican Church near the Inns of Court in the city, where George had had his Chambers. Police had to be there in force to control the crowds, particularly the press. As was expected, the young and beautiful wife of the young barrister, Penelope, slain on the orders of the gangster, Fordham – as was now generally known – was the main focus of the cameras.

She was driven to the funeral in a big black mourning car with George and Harriet, dressed in full mourning, silent and still. After the long and sombre service, receiving the condolences of so many important people she had never met before, she was like a beautiful marble statue, tall and rigidly straight, extending her gloved hand and murmuring her 'thank you' again and again, but otherwise silent.

It was only when the junior barrister, Greg Sheridan, who had been George's Junior in the trial and his close friend, came and took her hand, had the façade cracked a little. For a moment, Penny's face had begun to crumple as she said brokenly, "Oh, Greg! How can I bear it?" Then she straightened her back, the face still again and turned to the next person in the line. Annie looking on, was torn between grief and admiration, for her daughter.

Watching Penny in her total black clothing and mourning veil, Annie thought she was seeing a glimpse of her own mother, the Lady Mary, in similar situations, and marvelled at the composure of her little girl, only twenty – and now a widow.

The day after the big event, which appeared in every newspaper with dozens of photos accompanying the article, there was another funeral. This one was a very modest, private affair and attracted no attention at all. Only three mourners attended: Annie, Hannah Kelly and Sally Flinders. Mr Norman held a brief service and the body of Jean Harris was lowered into the ground. The parents kept their hostility and venom intact and did not put in an appearance.

Annie took Mr Norman and Sally Flinders back home for a cup of tea afterwards, but Hannah had to hurry back to the farm; the two new Land Army Girls were arriving that afternoon. The soldiers from Wembley Hospital who had been helping out, would no longer be coming to help with the milking – much to Sally's dismay.

She and the 'Spike' boy, who still wore a calliper on his leg, had begun a very serious and sober courtship – as befitted a good American young man who was a fully committed Southern Baptist.

Hannah smiled at the transformation of Sally – remembering her attitude to the Kelly's piety in the past – and looked on with approval. She was also delighted that Sally had asked to be permitted to stay on as well, so it seemed, for the first time in decades, that Hannah would begin to get some relief from the back-breaking work of the dairy.

* * *

After the funerals much was happening in the little village. The Seymours had gone – Elise and her two remaining children had left, without a word, one night. What she had arranged for the funeral of her son, no one knew; he was not buried locally. The house was to be sold.

George and Harriet, first asking Annie's advice, decided to buy the house for their daughter-in-law, Penelope. She would then be close to her mother and back again in her own area among friends. Until this occurred, she would be staying with her in-laws in their house.

With the arrests of Alan Darcy and Toby Moore, two bread-winners had left families behind to be fed and cared for. Annie was anxious about Rosemary Darcy and eventually persuaded Cassandra Perry to give the girl a trial, as a nursery maid.

Annie did not pretend that Rosemary had any proper experience, nor could she really guarantee she would be reliable, but it was worth a try. Cassandra not only agreed, but promised to teach the girl, all she knew about caring for young children. She also promised Annie she would do her best to help the poor, neglected child in every way she could. Annie especially stressed Rosemary needed help with manners, deportment, dressing and speech.

Molly Moore was a different problem. She now needed a full time job, and that meant that she also needed a baby sitter, until she would arrive home from work. Betty Johnson, at Annie's request, was willing to give Molly a full time job as cook, at the pub, doing the lunches and dinners each day, while Ada Cookson was only too glad to earn some extra money as a baby sitter – now that Alf was a permanent invalid.

Poor Mrs Liveridge was a problem. Annie was at her wits' end trying to think how to help that poor woman's situation, in a practical manner. After considering the matter carefully she took herself to her friend Florence Armitage.

As Annie explained to Florence, 'it was not a matter of trying to find Lily a job; she already had one – washing-up and cleaning at the pub – but it was the whole matter of her front room furniture'. Annie went on to point out, if the whole lot had to be taken back by the Receivers – as the results of crime – then poor Lily would be left with a bare house, as well as no husband. Annie had wondered if it were possible to *buy* the goods at the proper price, to enable Lily to have something left out of the wreck of her whole life of drudgery.

Florence appeared to be not listening; she was admiring yet again the wonderful way her infant smiled at his mother's face. Annie didn't like to tell her it was simply wind; instead, tactfully, agreed that the baby boy would undoubtedly grow up to be most handsome young man in the world; how could it not be so with such a beautiful mother?

Florence had known Annie for many years. She looked up smiling: "All right, Annie Watson, I'm well aware you're up to something with all that blarney." She laughed. "I also know that look! All right, *how much*?"

"I don't honestly know, Florrie. I've never had the money to buy such stuff myself. It could be more than … £100."

Florence called out. "Lucy, get me my cheque book would you? It's on the dressing table in my bedroom."

And so Lily was able to keep her furniture and a little of her pride left. The poor old woman dutifully travelled the very long distance out to Long Bay Goal to see 'her Bert' every visiting day, which fortunately was held on a Sunday, the only day she had off work.

Annie had also visited poor Charlie Munroe. He was a shadow of his former self; even his starched collar was limp. He had kept the store closed, ever since that terrible Sunday morning of Eric's arrest.

"I'll never be able to face anyone in the village again, Miss Anne," Charlie wrung his hands in distress. "What I'm to do, I don't really know. The farmers are knocking on the door all day, but I can't, I simply can't, face them."

"Oh course, you will face them and I'll help you, Charlie. I don't know a damn thing about your merchandise, but I can certainly take the money and give change and all that rubbish. What you need is a good strong lad to help you and I know exactly the one to bring you. But," Annie warned him, "don't open the store until I bring the boy and we'll face the people together."

Annie dashed off up the street to the Darcy house and brought Oliver to Charlie; she explained to the boy that he would be given the chance to work there after school each day and all day Saturday. For that, he would receive seventeen shilling and six pence. Oliver was thrilled.

He didn't intend to stay much longer at school – just the compulsory fourteen years and nine months, while now he could learn the Produce business for nothing *and* get paid for it, as well! His ghastly mother, realising that yet another one of her children would be earning, was only too anxious for him to take the offered position and, privately, threatened to flog him if he 'mucked it up.'

To Annie's surprise and delight, the boy did well, while Charlie, with a young chap to teach and supervise, was so busy he forgot to cringe whenever anyone spoke to him. Within a few days, with the boy helping him, the store was back in business, and Annie was able to leave her position as honorary sales assistant and return to her garden which was terribly neglected.

* * *

Billy had arrived home for end of term vacation. He had been shocked and horrified by the murder of George McKenzie, his brother-in-law; Annie had feared once again for him. However, as usual, Billy had bounced back again and was looking forward to this period of relaxation from the relentless grind of his university work.

Billy and his mother toured the garden and the orchard. The young man was appalled at the state of the garden; it had been their joint pride and joy.

"Mother," Billy dramatically exclaimed, "what in Heaven's name have you been doing? It's terrible!"

"I've been busy," Annie mumbled.

"Doing what?" was the stern voice of the embryonic don.

"Oh, this and that," Annie answered vaguely, "nothing much, son," Annie was anxious to change the subject. She took Billy's hand. "Bother the old garden, son, we'll soon sort that out now you're home. Come and have a cup of tea, while you tell me all about your second exciting term at university."

Soon Annie and Billy were chatting together. Well, Billy was doing most of the talking. When there was a lull in the conversation, Annie asked:

"Billy, are there many girls doing Classics?"

"No, not a great number, but I've met a wonderful girl – she's in the year ahead of me; an absolute whiz at Greek."

"A nice girl, son?"

"Very nice. Do you know what, Mum? She only came to speak to me when Professor Goldstein told her I was your son. Apparently he was an old beau of yours."

"A thin, stooped man, buck teeth, big ears and no chin, stutters when he speaks?"

"That doesn't sound very nice, Mum, but I suppose it's correct. You remember him?"

Annie shuddered slightly. "You can say that again, son," Annie's eyes narrowed. "Why did he tell this girl about me?"

"She's his daughter; she was so interested to hear that you were Lady Mary's daughter. We became friends after that; strange she wouldn't speak to me before."

"She sounds charming, son," Annie remarked dryly. "What is her name?"

"You won't believe it, but her name is Jael! You know, as in Jael and Sisera in the Old Testament."

"*Jael? …Jael!*

"Yes, that's right," Billy answered. Annie paused, then her face darkened.

"She's not handy with a hammer, is she son?"

"A hammer? … *Mother*! …You're outrageous! *That's a terrible thing to say!* Jael *killed* Sisera."

Annie, unmoved, took another arrowroot biscuit from the tin. With her face utterly expressionless, she remarked, dryly:

"Umm. Why …so she did, son, so she did."

ABOUT THE AUTHOR

Tony Brennan, completing Post Graduate University degrees, lectured in English Literature for some years and tutored in Abnormal Psychology. He wrote for Academic Journals and then turned to Fiction. His first book of Short Stories, 'It There Anyone There?' was published by Ginninderra Press in 2016 while his second collection of Short Stories has now been released. His writings range from a six-part Historical Crime Murder series – of which the first five books have been published while the sixth is with the publisher – to monographs on Hopkins' poetry. He is an occasional writer for an American newspaper and lives in Sydney, Australia.